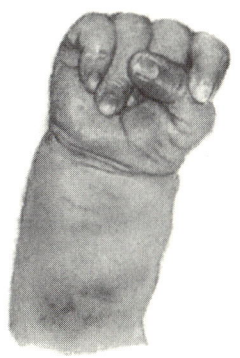

New York City, Summer/Fall 2000
Number Eleven

SHERMAN ALEXIE

THE TOUGHEST INDIAN IN THE WORLD

"**Bold, raucous, and sexy** . . . Alexie reveals himself to be a more fearless writer than one might ever have imagined."
— *San Francisco Chronicle Book Review*

"Fiercely compassionate and compellingly human, *The Toughest Indian in the World* is **Alexie at his finest**." — *The New York Post*

"Lyrical, rebellious, **sometimes funny, sometimes heartbreaking** . . . where Indians find themselves between worlds, between lives and between loves." — *The Denver Post*

 Atlantic Monthly Press
Distributed by Publishers Group West

OPEN CITY BOOKS
presents a new arrival
from an unknown place in
American fiction...

Venus Drive

by Sam Lipsyte

"Pitch perfect . . . *Venus Drive* explores the complexity of despair with poignancy and sly wit."   —*The New York Times Book Review*

"Lipsyte summons grace and beauty from the strangest places in the subdivision."   —*BOMB*

"Sam Lipsyte is a wickedly gifted writer . . . a collection that represents the emergence of a very strong talent."   —Robert Stone

"The new world as viewed by the newest."   —James Purdy

"These are torqued-up, enthusiastically black-hearted stories by a grimly cheerful author . . . Bukowski meets Paley.   —Padgett Powell

Available at bookstores nationwide or by sending a check or money order for $13.00 payable to Open City, Inc., 225 Lafayette Street, Suite 1114, New York, NY 10012.

Sam Lipsyte was born in New York City in 1968 and grew up in New Jersey. He is a former editor of *Feed*, and the former frontman for the noise rock band, Dungbeetle. His writing has appeared in *The Quarterly*, *5_Trope*, *Nerve*, *Aedon*, *Mother Jones*, *Spin*, and *Open City* magazine.

this summer

BOOKFORUM

the book review for art, fiction, & culture

on newsstands now

michael ondaatje *interviewed by* jonathan lethem
vivian gornick *on* saul bellow
david thomson *on* luis buñuel
greil marcus *on* philip roth
lynne tillman *on* the history of shit
rick moody *on* anne carson
david gates *on* allen ginsberg
jonathan bing's fiction forecast

guest fiction editor
jonathan lethem

subscribe to
BOOKFORUM
2 years 8 issues **$12**
1 800 966 2783

OPEN CITY

CONTRIBUTORS' NOTES	12	
VESTAL McINTYRE	27	Octo
GREG MILLER	51	Intercessor
ADAM CVIJANOVIC	53	Icepaper #3
SIOBHAN REAGAN	61	Neck, 17.5"
MICHAEL TAUSSIG	69	My Cocaine Museum
MARTIN G. LARRALDE	87	Art Project
PETER BAKOWSKI	95	Two Poems
LUCY CAVENDISH	101	Portrait of an Artist's Studio
BILL BROUN	111	Heart Machine Time
MARGARET RICKETTS	119	Devil's Grass
ENA SWANSEA	121	A Set for an Opera About Plants
JOHN McNALLY	125	The First of Your Last Chances
JODY WINER	141	Two Poems
LAURA RESEN	145	Art Project
ANDREA REISING	153	LaSalle
MELISSA PRITCHARD	155	Virgin Blue
EDWARD MYCUE	171	But the Fifties Really Take Me Home
JOANNA KIRK	173	Clara
HARVEY SHAPIRO	185	Four Poems
SEBASTIEN de GANAY	189	Überfremdung
GREGOR von REZZORI	199	On the Cliff
LETTERS	241	

LINCOLN PLAZA CINEMAS

Six Screens

63rd Street & Broadway
opposite Lincoln Center
757-2280

Summer Group Show

9 JUNE – 21 JULY · 534 WEST 21

SUMMER HOURS: MON – FRI 10 – 5

AUGUST BY APPOINTMENT

Meg Webster

9 SEPT – 14 OCT · 534 WEST 21

Group Show

9 SEPT – 14 OCT · 521 WEST 21

Carl Andre

21 OCT – 18 NOV · 521 WEST 21

Zoe Leonard

21 OCT – 18 NOV · 534 WEST 21

PAULA COOPER GALLERY

521/534 WEST 21ST STREET NEW YORK NY 10011 TEL 212 255 1105 FAX 212 255 5156

*m*icrowave, two

September-November 2000

123 Watts Gallery

123 Watts Street, New York, NY 10013 Tel: 212 219 1482 Fax: 212 274 1726
Open: Tues - Sat 12 - 6pm gallery@tribecatech.com   www.123watts.com

OPEN CITY

EDITORS
Thomas Beller
Daniel Pinchbeck

PUBLISHER
Robert Bingham

MANAGING EDITOR
Joanna Yas

ART DIRECTOR
Nick Stone

EDITOR-AT-LARGE
Adrian Dannatt

CONTRIBUTING EDITORS
Sam Brumbaugh
Amanda Gersh
Laura Hoffmann
Kip Kotzen
Jim Merlis
Geoffrey O'Brien
Elizabeth Schmidt
Alexandra Tager
Jon Tower
Lee Smith
Piotr Uklanski
Jocko Weyland

EDITORIAL ASSISTANTS
Aaron Balkan
Alicia Bergman

A four-issue subscription is $32 in the U.S.; $40 for institutions; $36 in Canada and Mexico; $52 in all other countries. Make checks payable to: OPEN CITY, Inc., 225 Lafayette Street, Suite 1114, New York, NY 10012. For credit card orders, see our Web site: www.opencity.org. E-mail: editors@opencity.org.

Cover photograph: *An F/A-18 Hornet emerges from a cloud caused when it broke the sound barrier in the skies over the Pacific Ocean, July 7, 1999.*
(AP Photo/Ensign John Gay/U.S. Navy)

Art projects in this issue curated by Adrian Dannatt.

Printed in the U.S.A.   ISBN 1-890447-22-6
Copyright © 2000 by Open City, Inc. All rights reserved.   ISSN 1089-5523

```
NASTY LITTLE MAN PUBLIC RELATIONS
           15 MAIDEN LANE
              8TH FLOOR
           NEW YORK,  NY
               10038
           (212) 343-2314
        FAX: (212) 343-0196
           info@nlmpr.com
```

Reservations 965-1414
Bakery & Restaurant 965-1785

80 Spring Street ~ NEW YORK ~ NY 10012

OPEN CITY

CONTRIBUTORS' NOTES

PETER BAKOWSKI was born premature with a hole in the heart in Melbourne, Australia. In the 1980s he bought a one-way ticket to London and was on the road for seven years. He composes all his poems on a Brother AX250 electric typewriter using one finger only. As his poems continue to appear in literary magazines in some fourteen countries he is reluctant to change this method.

BILL BROUN's "Heart Machine Time" is from an unpublished collection of stories about various addicts called *The Happy People Are Safe*. Other stories from this manuscript have appeared recently in *The Kenyon Review* and *The Indiana Review*. A graduate of the University of Houston's creative writing program, he works as a journalist in London, and is a frequent contributor to the *Times Literary Supplement*.

LUCY CAVENDISH was born in 1973 in Cumbria, England. Her work has been exhibited at the Bartley Drey Gallery and the European Academy for the Arts, both in London. She currently lives in New York City.

ADAM CVIJANOVIC is a painter based in New York City. The first in his series of hand-painted wallpapers, *Monument Valley*, was exhibited at Richard Anderson Gallery in 1999. An eighty-foot length of that paper is currently part of the "Landscape 2000" show at the University of Wisconsin. *Icepaper #3* is one of a series of studies for a full-scale polar paper that is anticipated by early 2001.

SEBASTIEN de GANAY commutes between the Château de Fleury outside Paris, the Schloss Petronell outside Vienna, and the family estancia in Argentina. He has exhibited with Richard Salmon in London, Jacqueline Moussion in Paris, and is currently represented by Galerie H.S. Steinek in Vienna. His exhibition "Überfremdung" was a deliberate response to the recent election campaign in Austria.

JOANNA KIRK is a London-based artist who has been working with pastel on paper since 1982. She has received commissions from Credit Suisse and is in numerous international collections including Saatchi and the Arts Council of Great Britain. Recent exhibitions include the Armory Show in New York; the Künstlerhaus Palais Thurn und Taxis in Bregenz, Austria; and Ciocca Arte Contemporanea, Milan. She is represented by Modern Art, Inc. in London.

MARTIN G. LARRALDE is an Argentine artist living and working in New York. After a large series of historical drawings, in 1977 he started a conceptual and non-categorizable oeuvre in various media. In 1998 he had an individual show with Annina Nosei Gallery, where he displayed paintings and drawings sometimes installed on furniture. These paintings depict a person, tree, animal, or furniture with a minimum as a rule, and the necessary as a condition. In Italy he exhibited in Galleria Alessandro Seno and has forthcoming shows in Padova and Modena.

JOHN McNALLY's short-story collection *Troublemakers* won the John Simmons Short Fiction Award and will be published by the University of Iowa Press in October 2000. He is the editor of two anthologies: *High Infidelity: 24 Great Short Stories about Adultery* (William Morrow), and *The Student Body: Short Stories about College Students and Professors*, to be published by the University of Wisconsin Press in 2001.

VESTAL McINTYRE was born and raised Nampa, Idaho, and attended Tufts University. He now lives in New York City.

GREG MILLER holds the Stewart Family Chair in Languages and Literature and serves as chair of the English Department at Millsaps College in Jackson, Mississippi. Miller's first book of poems, *Iron Wheel*, was published by the University of Chicago Phoenix Poets Series in 1998.

EDWARD MYCUE is a poet living in San Francisco. His recent books include *Night Boats* and *Because We Speak the Same Language.* His poems have appeared in *Lungfull*, *Hanging Loose*, *Fence*, and *Baker Street Irregulars.*

MELISSA PRITCHARD is the author of two story collections, *Spirit Seizures*, which received the Flannery O'Connor Award, and *The Instinct for Bliss*, which received the Janet Heidinger Kafka Award, as well as two novels, *Phoenix* and *Selene of the Spirits*. Fiction from a forthcoming collection has appeared recently in *The Paris Review*, *Boulevard*, *The Gettysburg Review*, and is forthcoming in *Prize Stories 2000: The O. Henry Awards*. She teaches in the creative writing program at Arizona State University.

SIOBHAN REAGAN's first published story, "Ambassadors," appeared in *Open City* Number Five in 1997. "Neck, 17.5"" is part of a novel.

ANDREA REISING is a visual artist and writer living in New York City. She was born in 1978 in Milwaukee, Wisconsin.

LAURA RESEN is an artist based in Paris and New York. These images of modernist Catholic structures are the first part of a project portraying the monothestic religions of the world, the next stage of which will be a sound sculpture addressing the Reformation. She is currently creating a one-person pemanent installation for the hotel 60 Thompson in Soho.

GREGOR von REZZORI was born in the Bukovina in 1914, which at the time was an outpost of the Austro-Hungarian Empire and is now a region divided between Ukraine and Romania. In 1969 *The New Yorker* published his story, "Memoirs of an Anti-Semite," which subsequently appeared as a section of a novel of the same name in 1979. His other books include *The Death of My Brother Abel* and *The Snows of Yesteryear*. He died in 1998 in Italy.

MARGARET RICKETTS is a poet and journalist from Berea, Kentucky. Her writing has appeared in *Wind: The Sun and Writing Who We Are,* a feminist poetry anthology. She currently works and studies at the University of Kentucky.

HARVEY SHAPIRO is the author of ten books of poetry, the latest of which is *Selected Poems*, published by Wesleyan University Press. He works as a consulting editor at *The New York Times Magazine.*

ENA SWANSEA is a painter from North Carolina. She lives in New York City where she shows with Robert Miller Gallery.

MICHAEL TAUSSIG teaches Daniel Pinchbeck about sorcery and other arcane aspects of anthropology including Walter Benjamin's *Arcades Project*. He has visited Colombia yearly since 1969 and is the author of several books including *Shamanism, Colonialism, and the Wild Man: A Study in Terror and Healing*; *The Nervous System*; *Mimesis and Alterity*; *The Magic of the State*; and *Defacement*.

JODY WINER lives in New York City. Her poems have appeared in *Mudfish* and the *Harvard Crimson*. She was a semi-finalist in the 1999 Discovery/*The Nation* Poetry Contest.

soho's best kept secret!

new, used and rare **books and records** at the lowest prices in town

cafe: full menu, beer and wine, catering **readings & special events**

Our entire inventory of books and records is donated. 100% of our profits go to provide services for homeless people living with AIDS and HIV.

housingworks
usedbookcafe

126 **crosby** st.
new york, ny 10012
(212) 334-3324

store hours
mon-wed: 10am-8pm   thurs, fri: 10am-9pm
sat: 12pm-9pm   sun: 12pm-7pm

rent our space

Klemens Gasser & Tanja Grunert, Inc.

524 West 19th Street
New York, NY 10011

Eija-Liisa Ahtila
Gunter Brus
Charlie Cho
Bart Domburg
VALIE EXPORT
Jitka Hanzlova
Peter Land
Thomas Locher
Helen Mirra
Rudi Molacek
Hanno Otten
Smith/Stewart
Elise Tak
Peter Zimmermann

Phone: (+1) 212 807 9494
Fax: (+1) 212 807 6594
e-mail: gasser@dti.net

resurrection
vintage clothing

123 E. 7th Street
NYC, 10009
212 228 0063

217 Mott Street
NYC, 10012
212 625 1374

8006 Melrose Avenue
LA, CA 90046
323 651 5516

DSL　　　1SERVER　　　COLO

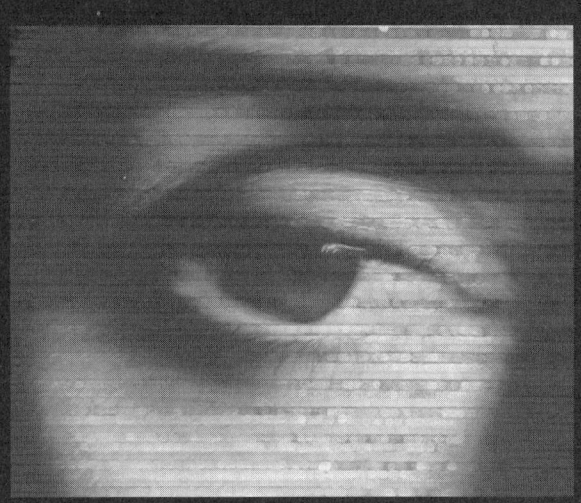

[DIGITAL TELEMEDIA]

WWW.DTI.NET
800-363-3428

OPEN CITY

Arty, classy, hip, and edgy.
—NEW YORK PRESS

Surprisingly funny and fresh.
—HARPER'S BAZAAR

Ambitiously highbrow.
—THE NEW YORK TIMES

Takes the old literary format and revitalizes it for a new generation's tastes.
—LIBRARY JOURNAL

SUBSCRIBE

4 issues for $32: Make checks payable to *OPEN CITY, Inc.* and mail to:
OPEN CITY 225 Lafayette Street, Suite 1114, New York, NY 10012
For credit card orders, see www.opencity.org

OPEN CITY
back issues

Make an investment in your future...
In today's volatile marketplace you could do worse.

Stories by Mary Gaitskill, Hubert Selby Jr., Vince Passaro. Art by Jeff Koons, Ken Schles, Devon Dikeou. (Vastly overpriced at $200, but fortunately we've had some takers. Only twenty-eight copies left.)

Stories by Martha McPhee, Terry Southern, David Shields, Jaime Manrique, Kip Kotzen. Art by Paul Ramirez-Jonas, Kate Milford, Richard Serra. (Ken Schles found the negative of our cover girl on 13th St. and Avenue B. We're still looking for the girl. $100)

Stories by Irvine Welsh, Richard Yates, Patrick McCabe. Art by Francesca Woodman, Jacqueline Humphries, Chip Kidd, Allen Ginsberg, Alix Lambert. Plus Alfred Chester's letters to Paul Bowles. (Our cover girl now has long brown hair. $150)

Stories by Cyril Connolly, Thomas McGuane, Jim Thompson, Samantha Gillison, Michael Brownstein, Emily Carter. Art by Julianne Swartz and Peter Nadin. Poems by David Berman and Nick Tosches. Plus Denis Johnson in Somalia. (A monster issue, sales undercut by slightly rash choice of cover art by editors. Get it while you can! $15)

Change or Die
Stories by David Foster Wallace, Siobhan Reagan, Irvine Welsh. Jerome Badanes's brilliant novella, "Change or Die" (film rights still available). Poems by David Berman and Vito Acconci. Plus Helen Thorpe on the murder of Ireland's most famous female journalist, and Delmore Schwartz on I. S. Eliot's squint. (A must-have at only $15!)

The Only Woman He's Ever Left
Stories by James Purdy, Jocko Weyland, Strawberry Saroyan. Michael Cunningham goes way uptown. Poems by Rick Moody, Deborah Garrison, Monica Lewinsky, Charlie Smith. Art by Matthew Ritchie, Ellen Harvey, Cindy Stefans. Rem Koolhaas Project. With a beautiful cover by Adam Fuss. (Only $10 for this blockbuster. Free to the first six people who request it.)

The Rubbed Away Girl
Stories by Mary Gaitskill, Bliss Broyard, and Sam Lipsyte. Art by Jimmy Raskin, Laura Larson, and Jeff Burton. Poems by David Berman, Elizabeth Macklin, Steve Malkmus, and Will Oldham. (A reader from Queens chastises us for our shameful synergistic moment with indie rock. $10)

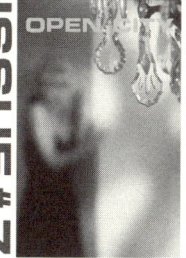

Beautiful to Strangers
Stories by Caitlin O'Connor Creevy, Joyce Johnson, and Amine Zaitzeff. Poems by Harvey Shapiro, Jeffrey Skinner, and Daniil Kharms. Art by Piotr Uklanski, David Robbins, Liam Gillick, and Elliott Puckette. Look for Zaitzeff's *Westchester Burning* in stores soon. ($10)

Bewitched
Stories by Jonathan Ames, Said Shirazi, and Sam Lipsyte. Essays by Geoff Dyer and Alexander Chancellor, who hates rabbit. Poems by Chan Marshall and Edvard Munch on intimate and sensitive subjects. Art projects by Karen Kilimnick, Maurizio Cattelan, and M.I.M.E. (Oddly enough, our bestselling issue. $10)

Editors' Issue
Previously demure editors publish themselves. Enormous changes at the last minute. Stories by Robert Bingham, Thomas Beller, Daniel Pinchbeck, Joanna Yas, Adrian Dannatt, Kip Kotzen, Amanda Gersh, Jocko Weyland. Poems by Tony Torn. Art by Nick Stone, Meghan Gerety, and Alix Lambert. ($10)

Please send a check or money order payable to *OPEN CITY, Inc.* Don't forget to specify the issue number and give us your address. Send checks to:

OPEN CITY
225 Lafayette Street, Suite 1114, New York, NY 10012

For credit card orders, see www.opencity.org

TRANSITION

Never dull

Subscribe on line at www.TransitionMagazine.com

FEED

www.feedmag.com

Contributors include:

Sam Lipsyte, author of Venus Drive

Geoff Dyer, National Book Award finalist

Roger Ebert, "Roger Ebert & The Movies"

Alex Ross, The New Yorker music critic

Sven Birkerts, author of The Gutenberg Elegies

Denise Caruso, New York Times columnist

Lisa Carver, author of Dancing Queen

Jenny Offill, author of Last Things

Esther Dyson, cyber-guru

And **FEED** Magazine co-founders Steven Johnson and Stefanie Syman

"Some of the sharpest writing on-line or off.... Unfailingly original, insightful and refreshing."
—The New York Times

LET THE SUN IN.

NOON

1369 MADISON AVENUE PMB 298 NEW YORK NEW YORK 10128-0711

SUBSCRIPTION $9 DOMESTIC AND $14 FOREIGN

Octo

Vestal McIntyre

ANGELFISH, BOXFISH, TWO SEA SNAILS, STRIPED GRUNT, SURGEON-fish, hermit crab—Octo ate them all. He outgrew the Sea Monkeys Jamie bought to feed him and he started eating the other fish. So Ma and Daddy say it's time to get rid of Octo.

Angelfish was the first to go. It disappeared. Jamie thought it might've got sucked into the filter and died. I've got to clean the filter, thought Jamie. But the angelfish was under Octo's mantle, being eaten. When Octo moved, a day later, there was wide-eyed angelfish, fins gone, jumbled bones, a strip of skin waving in time with the filter's bubbling. Jamie got the net. He flushed the angelfish. He didn't tell Ma or Daddy.

That stupid fish tank smells, said Rebecca.

Jamie, if you're going to have an aquarium you've got to keep it clean, said Ma.

But that was months ago. Now Octo's eaten everyone else, too. Now it's just Octo, sitting quietly, thinking.

Jamie tries to get Elsie help him make seawater, but she won't. Not in my job description, says Elsie. Elsie's the care provider. She's old and has a limp and can't work. She gets more money from the government if she comes for an hour on the days when everyone else is at work or school. She makes lunch and gives Jamie pills. She's from Queens. Sometimes she stays longer than an hour if Jamie gets her talking. Like the Monday after the weekend when Jamie first got Octo.

Look Elsie! said Jamie. He brought Elsie to the tank.

Whoa! She backed up.

Isn't it cute? Octo was teeny-little, swimming around the tank. He was the size of an umbrella you'd put in a tropical drink. He swam back and forth opening and closing his legs like a tiny umbrella.

I wouldn't say cute, said Elsie getting closer to the tank. But it's somethin. It sure is somethin. You sure you can keep that in a tank?

Jamie told her what the man at the store had told him: that Octo would only survive if the water is kept fresh. Jamie would have to siphon out a little every day and replace it. Otherwise, when Octo squirted ink like he did when Jamie first put him in, he would make the water poison and die.

What do you mean siphon out water? asked Elsie. Jamie tried to show her—he started sucking on the siphon to get it going—but Elsie had turned and walked to the kitchen saying, I can't watch this.

That day Elsie ended up telling Jamie about the giant octopus that was displayed at Coney Island when she was little. You had to pay the guy a quarter, right? And he lets you into this tent, this long, dimly-lit tent, and the minute you walk in you can smell the rot. Professor Whoever from Wherever is talkin about how he's traveled the world with this exquisite specimen. And laid out on this big piece of canvas was this dead octopus, half rotted away. Musta been fifty feet long.

Was it real? asked Jamie.

Sure it was. If it was fake it woulda smelled a whole lot better.

It must have been a giant squid, said Jamie.

You going to eat that orange or not? It's good for you.

I'm gonna eat it.

Octopus, squid, what's the difference? said Elsie. Jamie tried to tell her but she just went on. And there was the freakshow with the man with the stretchy skin and the bearded lady and all of that. Of course that's considered cruel nowadays. They don't have that kinda show.

They don't have it any more? said Jamie. He was disappointed.

Of course not, said Elsie.

Do they still have Coney Island?

You never been to Coney Island? What are you talkin, a kid like you?

No.

Elsie shook her head and picked up Jamie's plate. Where they keepin you?

That day Elsie stayed a full two hours. When she pulled on her coat she said, What am I doin, staying so long. You think I get paid extra for this? No sir-ee I do not.

That was when Octo was tiny, when he was still satisfied with tiny brine shrimp. Later, when Octo got sea snail number one, Daddy laughed.

Damn thing's goin after its *own* now, said Daddy. Mean mother. Thinks he's a big shot.

It wasn't a little snail. It was giant. Jamie would follow it around the tank. Its soft part made an oval against the glass, and Jamie would watch it up close, seeing its tiny mouth open and close, littler than a freckle, going wow, wow, wow, eating its way so slow around the tank. One morning snail number one was a bump under the brown web between Octo's two front legs. Octo wasn't moving. The black bars in Octo's eyeballs watched Jamie. You're eating one of the sea snails, aren't you? said Jamie. Octo looked but never blinked. His eyes were always wide open. If my eyes were that wide open, I'd look scared or wondering, thought Jamie. But Octo never looks scared or wondering. He just looks like he knows.

Two days later, in the corner of the tank was a pile of the snail shell in three pieces.

That Octopus eat one of them snails? said Elsie. She never got too close to the tank. She always scowled when she talked about Octo.

Yeah. I think so, said Jamie. Look. He piled up the pieces in the corner. It's like when I eat peanuts.

Ugh! said Elsie. You oughta get rid of that thing. It ate the angelfish, too.

I'm not getting rid of Octo, said Jamie.

That night Daddy said, Damn thing's going after its *own* now.

What's that? said Ma. She was feeding Jacob.

The monster ate one of them snails, said Daddy.

Not a monster, said Jamie.

That thing . . . said Ma.

I hate it! said Rebecca.

Shut up! said Jamie.

You shut up, said Rebecca.

You both shut up and eat, said Daddy.

I don't see why Jamie gets to keep that stinky thing and I don't get to have a dog! said Rebecca.

Yeah! Dog! said Nancy.

Shut up, said Jamie.

Jamie gets the aquarium because he's the oldest, said Ma. When you turn thirteen we'll think about letting you get a dog.

That is so unfair! said Rebecca.

Until then, said Ma, there's no use in whining about it.

That is so unfair! I hate this! He gets whatever he wants!

Do not, said Jamie.

Now listen you two, said Daddy.

Yes*sir*, said Rebecca. You get whatever you want just because you're a boy and you're stupid.

Becca! said Ma.

I am *not* stupid, said Jamie.

All right, said Daddy. He was standing up.

Nancy was crying now.

I hate this place! said Rebecca twisting out of her chair. I *hate* it! The chair fell over and she ran off.

Becca! yelled Daddy walking after her.

Now Jamie, settle down, said Ma moving toward him. Don't cry honey.

Nancy wailed.

Jacob banged his tray.

Jamie hush now, please honey, don't cry. Ma's hands were on Jamie's shoulders.

Judith! Daddy yelled from the other room. Will you shut him up?

Hush sweetheart.

Nancy was crying.

Judith!

I am not stupid, said Jamie.

Shh-shh-shh.

Now that all the others are eaten, Jamie feeds Octo dead shrimp from the store. Ma lets him.

Octo doesn't move much now. For one thing he's too big. His legs are the length of the tank, and then some. They reach the far end then coil against the glass. The coils twitch. He heaves in, stops, then his funnel opens and water billows out, pushing aside the blue gravel till there's a bare spot. Sometimes he gets up and his skin turns into spines and he glides to a different corner. For a few seconds every part of him is flushed pink, coiling and uncoiling, then he's still again.

He's bored, thinks Jamie, plopping a shrimp into the tank. He likes eating live things better. The shrimp flutters down and lands on one of the coils. Octo doesn't move, but his eyes now watch the shrimp from across the tank. Nancy kneels down next to Jamie. Sit still, Nancy. Maybe he'll eat it while we're watching.

Octo breathes in . . . breathes out. Two legs begin to uncoil.

Rebecca passes behind Jamie and Nancy on the way to her room, then comes back and looks into the tank. Jamie can see her reflection in the glass. She puts her hands on her hips, all bratty.

Is that thing eating?

Shhhh! say Jamie and Nancy. Octo has turned the underside of two legs toward the shrimp. Now the shrimp starts to inch up Octo's legs, being passed from one sucker to the next, toward his mouth.

I cannot even *tell* you guys how much that grosses me out, says Rebecca.

Octo freezes.

Shut up! whispers Jamie.

Go on, Becca, says Nancy. You're ruining it.

No problem! says Rebecca and she tosses her hair and marches off to her and Nancy's bedroom and closes the door behind her. Then her music comes on, loud.

Octo begins again, slowly passing the shrimp from sucker to sucker.

I don't think it's gross, whispers Nancy.

Good, whispers Jamie.

I like Octo.

Well I think he likes you, too.

Really? How can you tell?

Well, when he's scared he turns white, and when he's mad he turns red. But now he's his normal color. That means he's comfortable with you. He knows you like him, so he's not afraid.

You mean he can tell me from Rebecca or Ma?

Of course he can, Nancy.

And I'm the only one he likes?

Uh-huh . . . other than me . . . and maybe Elsie.
So can I always watch him eat?
Uh-huh.
Can I feed him?
No. I have to feed him.
Okay.

Without moving too much, Jamie puts his arm around Nancy. Octo freezes for a second, the shrimp already half under his mantle. Then he draws in the rest.

Jamie goes to the bathroom and makes seawater. Before dinner is when he's allowed, because no one else needs the bathtub. He fills the tub half-way, adds a teaspoon from the blue bottle to take away the chlorine, then adds a scoop of sea salt, pushes up his sleeves, and swishes the water with his hands. He drops in the little glass hydrometer to measure the saltiness, and leaves it for a while.

During dinner, Elsie calls and tells Ma she's still sick and won't come tomorrow. Ma will have to leave him his lunch and set out his pills again. Elsie was sick yesterday, too.

She's not quitting, is she? asks Jamie.
No, she's not quitting, says Daddy, she's just sick, right Ma?
I don't think she's quitting, Jamie.
Jamie would be sad if Elsie quit.

Gloria, the caretaker before Elsie, had quit. Jamie had fired Rita, the one before Gloria, because he hated her. She was always late and hardly talked to him and made the same thing every day—macaroni and cheese and an apple. Jamie's proud of this. I fired her, he likes to say. Before Rita, Jamie used to go to school during the mornings at Empire State Developmental Center. He got kicked out because of his Fits of Rage. He's glad, though. He couldn't stand going to school with retards. Now that his Fits of Rage have stopped they might send him back. But he'd rather stay home.

After dinner, he checks the hydrometer in the bathtub. The water is just right so he takes a bucket to the living room. He sucks on the siphon to get it going and accidentally takes in a salty mouthful. He spits it into the empty bucket. Then he gently pours in some new water as old water runs through the siphon, filling the empty bucket.

Octo watches him calmly. He's used to all this.

Late that night, Jamie has a dirty dream. He wakes up, and he's made a mess. This has happened before. The first time Ma said that it was okay. This kind of thing was supposed to happen, and it was nothing to cry about. She said next time he should go to the bathroom, clean up, and go back to bed. No big deal.

But Jamie can't help but feel ashamed. He holds his privates tight with both hands. The digital alarm clock says 12:23. He feels weak and he wants to cry. He wants to fast-forward time until he's clean again and back in bed and about to fall asleep.

He slips out of bed and shuffles into the dark hall, hunched over, still holding himself. He's careful not to make any noise—he doesn't want anyone to find him. Ma and Daddy's light is still on so he's extra-quiet as he passes their door. They're talking.

I'll take him to the docks at Williamsburg and we can dump it in the river. If he thinks it'll survive he won't get that upset.

Ron, there's no way we're going to do this without him throwing a fit. I just don't think it's worth it.

Well it has to happen sometime. The living room smells like shit, the thing is huge. Sure, it was cute for a while, he had somethin to be excited about, he was real responsible about it, but it's gotten way out of hand. You looked at it lately? It's huge! It must be fuckin miserable in that little tank.

I know, I know.

You just explain how sad Mr. Octopus is, Judith. Make him feel bad for keepin it in a tank when it could out in the ocean with its little sea friends . . .

Oh Ron, don't make a joke.

I'm not makin a joke. You explain it to him, and then the three of us will go for a little drive down to the river—Jamie, Pops, and the monster. Simple's that.

That's not going to work! That's not how Jamie thinks. He loves it. He doesn't talk about anything else.

All the more reason . . .

I know, all the more reason to get rid of it. It's not good for him anymore. All I'm saying is . . . I don't know. We just better be ready for a fight.

As Ma says this, her voice is louder and there are footsteps. Jamie runs back to his room and ducks behind the door. Ma opens her bedroom door and the hall is brighter. Then the bathroom door closes and he hears the sink running. Jamie tears off his pajamas, wipes himself with the shirt, and stuffs it under the other clothes in the hamper. He opens the bottom drawer carefully and pulls on clean pajamas. Then he curls up in bed, and pulls the covers over his head, trembling. The bathroom door opens, the light flicks off.

I'm made of rock, thinks Jamie. I'm a statue. He holds his breath. Ma's footsteps come down the hall, past her own door, to his.

Jamie? she whispers from his doorway.

He holds completely still.

She pauses. One onethousand, two onethousand, three onethousand. Then her feet pad away.

You can breathe again but don't cry. Don't cry don't cry don't cry. Four onethousand, five onethousand, six onethousand. Did she close her door?

He hears Ma close her bedroom door.

Don't cry don't cry.

He thinks of the things that usually put him to sleep.

He's in a treasure chest at the bottom of the ocean.

He's a baby chick still in its shell.

There's a secret about Octo that Ma and Daddy don't know. Octo once escaped from the tank.

It happened at about one o'clock on a Tuesday afternoon three weeks ago. Jamie had been looking at a comic book on his bed, waiting for Elsie, when he heard a loud bump come from the living room. Elsie? he called, but she usually buzzed once or twice to be let in before she used her key. Jamie ran to the living room and saw the tank tipped over on its side and water running across the stand and pouring down, turning the orange carpet brown. Octo was heaving himself across the carpet with his back legs, waving his two front legs before him. His body was pale, almost white. He reached the corner between the bookshelf and the wall, stopped, huddled into the corner and reached up, searching the wall with his front legs. He whipped them around the bookshelf and pulled down some books which fell open onto the floor.

Oh no, oh no, said Jamie, stomping the floor, not knowing what to do. He ran to the bathroom, started filling the tub with cool water, threw in a scoop of sea salt, then ran back to the living room. Octo had dragged himself along the wall to the sofa, coiled his legs around the sofa's feet, and was stuffing himself beneath.

Oh no! cried Jamie. He grabbed Octo's body and pulled. Octo turned from white to red at Jamie's touch and black ink dribbled onto the floor. Jamie had never felt Octo before. Octo's skin was sticky, and as Jamie pulled he felt like rubber. Oh please Octo, let go. Jamie quit pulling, knelt, and started unwrapping Octo's legs from the sofa's feet. Another of his legs coiled around Jamie's arm. Please, pleeeease, Jamie was crying now. Finally Octo gave up. His whole body relaxed and Jamie picked him up. He was much heavier than Jamie imagined. His legs dangled and tried to wrap around Jamie as he carried Octo to the bathroom and put him into the tub. Octo rippled red and white and again squirted ink at Jamie. He lunged away from the running water to the far end of the tub and gathered his legs in coils with the white suckers showing. I'm so sorry, Octo. Jamie hated to scare Octo so. Don't move, just sit still. Jamie turned off the water and ran back to the living room. He knew he had to settle himself down and get things cleaned up before Elsie came, but he couldn't stop crying. Stop crying! he said to himself and struck his fist hard against his thigh. Stop! Stop! Stop!

He righted the tank, replaced the cover and light which Octo had pushed onto the floor, and dragged it, stand and all, into the coat closet. He scooped up the gravel which had fallen onto the carpet and threw it in the kitchen trash. He went to the bathroom to get towels and Octo was still curled up, pale now, with dark rings around his eyes, and the water was murky with his ink. Just stay there. Everything's gonna be okay. Jamie grabbed three towels from the shelf, ran back to the living room and started mopping up the water on his hands and knees. It stunk and everything was still blurry even though he had stopped crying and his nose dripped and he didn't wipe it.

The buzzer buzzed.

Oh no. He quickly bunched up the towels and threw them into the closet. Then he went to the bathroom and looked at himself in the mirror. His eyes were red and wet and his hair was a mess. He washed his hands, splashed his face and flattened his hair.

The buzzer buzzed twice more impatiently.

Okay, Octo, just be quiet. Everything's okay.

35

He went back to the living room, but before he could buzz her in, he heard Elsie coming up the stairs.

Jamie? What's goin on? You okay?

Jamie undid the latches and opened the door for her. Yeah, I was just going to the bathroom.

You sure? You been cryin? She touched his chin and made him look her in the eye.

Nuh-uh.

Phew. Elsie wrinkled her nose and fanned herself with her hand. That pet of yours stinks to high heaven. I don't know why your parents... but she didn't finish because she knew it upset Jamie when she talked bad about Octo. She limped to the kitchen, without noticing the dark spot on the carpet in the corner, or that the tank was missing.

She opened the fridge and bent over. Bologna again? Or beans and franks?

Bologna, please, said Jamie sitting down at the kitchen table.

How's your Mom and Dad?

They're all right.

Yeah? They gettin along?

I guess.

You're lucky kid, you know that? To have a family that gets along. You should see my family. Get us all in one room, everybody's either yellin at each other or not speakin to each other. One or the other.

We don't always get along. We fight.

Take my little sis Sarah. She hasn't talked to her daughter for two years, *two years*, and ya know why? Because she married an Italian Roman Catholic. Two years! You know how long that is? It's torture for both of them, but they won't give in and call the other. I tell her, Sarah, you're missing out on your daughter and your beautiful grandson. He's gonna grow up not knowing you. Why do this to yourself? But she won't budge. So stubborn just like our father. Mayonnaise, right?

Right.

And mustard?

Right.

Anyways, so she won't budge. I tell her, you're a Jew livin in Bensonhurst. You run the risk. What do you expect? Now if I could show her your parents, maybe that would do somethin. Your mother's Jewish right?

Yeah.

And your father's an Italian Roman Catholic, right?

He's Italian.

And look, they get along, they live in this nice apartment, they have good-lookin kids . . .

Elsie pinched Jamie's cheek, but he didn't smile.

What's the matter kiddo? You're not talkin to me.

Jamie had only been half-listening to her. He had thought he heard a sloshing sound from the bathroom, then decided it was his imagination.

I don't know, he said. I don't feel good. I'm sick.

Well go lay down then. I'll call you when it's ready. You don't look so good. She put the back of her hand against his forehead. Go lay down. Rest. Go on.

On the way to his bedroom, Jamie peeked into the bathroom. Octo was still in the same position, but he had returned to his normal spotted pinkish-brown. Just a few more minutes, whispered Jamie and closed the door.

He lay on his bed, closed his eyes, and listened. Elsie began to sing in the kitchen. Jamie believed in the power of crossing fingers. He crossed his fingers on both hands and tried to cross his toes in his shoes. *Please don't go to the bathroom*, he said in his mind. *Don't even go in the living room. Just stay in the kitchen.* If she found Octo and saw the mess she would tell Ma and Daddy and they would hate Octo more than they already did. They might even decide he had outgrown the aquarium and make Jamie get rid of him. He imagined taking Octo back to the pet store. The man would be surprised to see how big Octo had gotten and he'd say it'd be easy to sell Octo to a new owner. He'd put Octo in a tiny tank, and Octo's frightened eyes would watch Jamie. He wouldn't understand why he was back here. What if the new owner didn't feed him right or change the water? Now Jamie was crying a little, just imagining it.

Elsie's singing burst through the kitchen door and into the hallway. Jamie crossed his fingers so tight his knuckles popped. The bathroom door slammed. Then Elsie screamed. Jamie screamed too. He ran to his doorway to see Elsie backing into the hall, clutching her chest with one hand and holding up her pants with the other.

Elsie! It's okay! He just got out and I haven't had a chance . . .

What in the hell? Elsie tucked in her big shirt and zipped up her pants. Scared the livin . . . Look at me. I'm shakin like a leaf. What in the hell is that thing doin in there, boy?

Don't tell, Elsie, please! He just got out and I had to put him somewhere till . . .

Got out? Oh God, I have to sit down.

Jamie followed her to the kitchen, tugging on her shirtsleeve. Please, Elsie, don't tell Ma and Daddy. It's nothing really. I just gotta put him back and everything'll be okay.

Quit pullin me, kid. Elsie sat down heavily at the kitchen table and put her palm to her forehead.

You're not gonna tell, are you Elsie?

Settle down. Just give me a second. You said it got out? What do you mean, it got out?

He just pushed the lid off his tank and crawled out.

Oh Jesus.

No, it's okay, Jamie wailed. He never did it before. I'll just stick the lid on tighter. Don't tell! Jamie clutched Elsie's arm and shook her.

Would you get off? Elsie pushed him. I won't tell, just settle down, kid. Quit cryin. I'm the one who just got the pee scared outta me.

So you won't tell?

No I won't tell. None of my business anyways.

Jamie sat down and wiped his eyes. Really?

Yeah. But you better clean it up. And if they ever do find out, I didn't know nothin and had nothin to do with it. You got that?

Yeah.

And you owe me one, kid. Now eat. I'm leavin. This place is too much for an old woman. Damn near gave me a heart attack.

Okay.

And don't go tellin your mother I left early either.

Okay.

Don't get paid to deal with this.

After she left, Jamie cleaned up. He sprayed disinfectant on the carpet. He went to the bathroom, dipped the bucket into the bathtub, and nudged Octo toward it. Octo calmly climbed in. He made all new water for the tank, and took bucketful after bucketful to the living room. It took all afternoon. He tested the water. Then, very carefully, he poured in Octo. He fastened the lid to the top of the tank with a few pieces of black electrical tape

Since then, Octo has never escaped, though Jamie sometimes finds him snaking one leg up to press against the lid.

Rebecca hasn't talked to Jamie or even looked at him for two days. She goes through these phases, when she's so sick of him she has to pretend he doesn't exist. If he says anything to her she gives him a dirty look or just turns and walks away.

This time she's mad because she's tired of sharing a room with Nancy. Jamie's always had his own room, she complained to Ma. Why can't *he* share for a while? Ma told her that Jamie is a teenager and needs his own space and went on about how he spends the whole day at home while she gets to go to school and to her friends' houses—talking like Jamie wasn't listening even though he was.

Two days went by, Rebecca not saying a word to Jamie. Then, on the third day, Rebecca comes home from school earlier than usual, before Ma and Daddy are home from work. Jamie's watching videos on TV. Rebecca sits down on the far end of the sofa. Jamie looks over. She stares at the TV, scowling.

Hi, says Jamie.

Rebecca looks at him calmly, then turns back to the TV. They sit in silence, then Rebecca says, You know, you could like, volunteer to share a room with Nancy. It's only fair.

Why should I?

'Cause! You've always had your own room, and I've always shared. I never get any privacy. I can't even talk on the phone in private. I'm either out here and everyone can hear me or I'm in there and Nancy's crawling all over my bed wanting me to play with her. I have to shut myself in the hall closet to have a simple conversation!

You can take the phone into my room if you want.

That's not enough! I want to have my own room! Look, we can trade off. I can have your room for a few months then you can have it back for a while, like that.

No. I need to be by myself.

Oh screw you, Jamie! You get everything you want and you just can't share, can you!

Screw *you!*

I hate you, you know that? Rebecca yells and throws a pillow across the sofa at Jamie. Sometimes I wish you'd just die!

Shut up! Shut up or I'll tell!

Screw you, you big baby! You are such a pain in my butt.

How am I a pain in your butt? I leave you alone. I don't even talk to you!

You don't even *know* how miserable you make me, Jamie. You should hear how the kids at school make fun of me! They say I have a retard brother and it must run in the family. I get that all the time because of you!

Jamie lunges at Rebecca, punching aimlessly. Rebecca shrieks, pushes him onto the ground and kicks him hard. He pulls her down, and they roll across the carpet, punching and slapping until Jamie's head strikes the leg of the coffee table. He lets out a hoarse bawl and digs his teeth into Rebecca's arm. She pushes and scratches his face until he lets go and curls into a ball.

I hate you! she screams. Her voice cracks and she bursts into tears. She hits him again and stands up. I hate you so much!

You're gonna feel bad later for saying that, Jamie whimpers.

No I won't! I'll never feel bad 'cause it's the truth and I'll never say I'm sorry! She stumbles away from Jamie.

He feels beneath his eye. There's a little blood.

Look what you did! he cries.

I don't care! She's standing beside Octo's tank, holding her arm where Jamie bit her. You're such a sissy! I can't believe you bit me! She glances down at Octo. You and your stupid ugly pet. She hits the glass with her fist and Octo glides to the opposite corner.

Leave him alone, says Jamie. He jumps to his feet and moves toward her.

Daddy's getting rid of that thing, you know, says Rebecca, backing away from Jamie into the hallway.

He is not!

Yes*sir!* I heard him tell Ma he's gonna pour Lysol in there and kill it.

What?

And she told him not to and he said it was the only way to get rid of it and you'd think it just died.

Liar! Jamie lunges for her but she runs into her bedroom, slams the door and locks it. Jamie pounds on the door. Liar! You're lying!

Am *not*, comes Rebecca's voice and she laughs meanly. Your stupid pet's dead!

Jamie howls and beats the door.

No response.

Rebecca! You're lying, aren't you! When did you hear that?

Rebecca is ignoring him now. She turns on her music, then starts to sing along. He pounds one more time then goes to his room, locks the door, and lays down, trembling. He thinks back to when Octo ate the hermit crab. It was the last one to go and the only one Jamie actually watched Octo eat.

He had been sitting by the tank watching the crab overturning gravel with it's scissor-claws, looking for food algae to eat. It was happier, Jamie thought, now that it didn't have to compete with the snails.

Suddenly, Octo pounced, covering the crab with his legs and quickly drawing it under his mantle. The crab scrambled under Octo for just a second, then it was still.

Wow, Jamie whispered to himself, and he thought, should I have stopped him? But how could I? He was so quick! Jamie had not known Octo could move so quickly.

Now, laying on his bed, Jamie thinks of how Octo fools everyone by being so calm. He spends his life sitting, watching, taking in what's going on, so everybody thinks that's all he can do. Then, when he needs to, he strikes quick like a snake.

Ma knocks on the door. Jamie?

I'm taking a nap, Ma.

Everything okay?

Yes. Go away, please.

Jamie lies on his bed thinking until Ma knocks again and says, Wake up, honey. Dinner's ready.

Okay. Just a minute.

He rolls out of bed, tucks in his shirt, and stands up straight. He walks out, down the hall, and into the dining room.

Jacob is laughing and smearing gravy across his face and kicking the legs of the high chair. Eat right, Jacob, says Ma who's spooning mashed potatoes onto her plate.

Daddy's cutting Nancy's roast beef for her and telling a story from work about how Johnny Rosso's gonna transfer to the Bronx rather than deal with the district supervisor, who everyone hates.

Mommy, why isn't Rebecca talking? whines Nancy.

Mind your own business, says Rebecca.

Is there something wrong, Rebecca? asks Ma.

No. Tell Nancy to mind her own business.

Jamie! says Ma. What's that on your face?

Everyone looks at Jamie who's standing in the doorway.

Huh?

You have a scratch on your cheek, honey, says Ma standing up. You're hurt.

Oh.

Ma holds his chin and looks close under his eye and says, There's dried blood. Who did this?

Everyone's watching except Rebecca who's frowning down at her plate.

Jamie says, Rebecca.

Rebecca doesn't look up.

You two had a fight? Is that what's wrong? said Ma turning toward Rebecca.

Rebecca shakes her head and quietly says, No.

Ma turns to Jamie, who says, We were just playin, Ma. It was an accident.

Ma licks a napkin and wipes hard under his eye. Too much roughhousing. You two should be careful.

Ow! Easy, Ma.

They sit down. Jamie eats quietly while Daddy goes on with his story. Ma alternates between listening to Daddy and cleaning up Jacob, who has settled down now and is shoving one spoonful of mashed potatoes after another into his mouth. Rebecca doesn't look up. Nancy glances from Jamie to Rebecca, then back to Jamie. She begins to cry quietly. After a minute, Ma notices.

Nancy, what's wrong?

Nancy sobs and big tears fall into her food.

Honey! What is it?

Nancy wipes her nose and between sobs says, Jamie and Becca hate each other.

Nancy, they don't hate each other, says Daddy.

Mind your own business, Nancy, says Rebecca.

Shush, Rebecca! says Ma, then to Nancy, Sweetheart, everything's all right.

Stop crying and eat, says Daddy.

It's okay, Nancy, says Jamie quietly because he's next to her. Shh.

Nancy doesn't stop crying, but wipes her face with her napkin and begins to eat again.

Jamie is surprised the next day when the buzzer buzzes at one o'clock and it's Elsie. She hasn't come since Monday, and it's Friday.

Elsie, you're back!

I'm back? Where'd I go? Just been a little sick.

Are you all better now?

I'm a little better. When you're my age you're never *all* better. How bout you? You been okay by yourself?

Yeah, Ma's been leavin lunch for me, and I just sit around and watch TV. Pretty boring. I thought maybe you'd quit, and Ma just hadn't told me.

Quit? Na. Why would I quit?

I don't know. I thought maybe you just got sick of me.

What are you talkin about? Sick of my little friend? Elsie shakes Jamie by the shoulders and he laughs. No way!

Elsie sits down at the kitchen table and Jamie tells her about how mean Rebecca was to him and about the fight. Telling the story makes his chest tighten and his eyes tear, but he stays calm, even when he gets to the part about Octo.

And she told me Daddy's gonna kill Octo. She said he's gonna poison him and not tell me a thing about it.

Poison him?

Yeah. Pour Lysol in his tank and kill him.

Sounds like your sister's making up stories.

You think so?

Jamie, your sister's havin a hard time. You gotta leave her alone when she wants to be left alone . . .

I *do!*

. . . and sometimes you gotta leave her alone even when she wants your attention, ya see? Once you prove she can't make you laugh or cry just like that, she'll start treatin you like a real person. Things'll be okay, kid. Wait and see. Elsie puts her hand on Jamie's shoulder and heaves herself up out of her chair. She goes to the fridge.

Jamie says, So last night I didn't dream about anything but Daddy killing Octo. I spent all morning checking where all the poisonous stuff is, like Lysol, bleach, fingernail-polish remover . . . sort of memorizing how everything's arranged under all the sinks.

Why?

So if I find Octo dead, and I see that the Lysol's gone or the bleach is in a different place, I'll know Daddy did it.

Jamie, you're dad's not gonna kill it. And if he did, then what? There are more important things . . .

At least I'd know, Elsie. I'd know he did it.

Elsie was quiet. Then she said again, There are more important things, kid. What happens if the octopus dies on its own, eh? I wouldn't be surprised. It's way too big for that tank. It hardly moves anymore. What then? You gonna blame your dad for that?

Not if he doesn't do it.

I'm just afraid you're gonna get all upset and blame him anyways. Just remember, kid, he's your dad. He wants what's best for you and you gotta respect that.

What if he doesn't *know* what's best for me? What if he does what's bad for me?

You gotta respect him still.

That's not fair.

But that's how it works.

Well . . . he doesn't want what's best for Octo. That's for sure.

Ah, what're we arguin over anyways? says Elsie, setting a bowl of soup in front of Jamie. Your dad's not gonna kill Octo.

But Elsie's wrong. Late that night, Jamie is going in and out of sleep. He can't get comfortable. In his dream he's in tentacles and branches and seaweed. He's holding his breath, then he gasps, surprised that he can breathe water. Now he's out of his dream and out of sleep and he kicks off his sheet cause it's hot. Now he's underwater again and the difference between being awake and being asleep doesn't make the same sense. He's at a wall of coral and he touches the surface. It's sticky. His hands stick. Then his nose burns at breathing bleach. Or is it just the thought of breathing bleach?

A bump from the living room yanks him out of sleep. He knows what it is, but he can't believe it—partly because he knew it would happen (and can never believe when those things actually happen), and partly because his head's only halfway out of the dream.

He's out of bed and stumbling down the hall and he hears Daddy's voice. *Shit . . . Shit!*

There's the tank, knocked to the floor, the glass broken like a spider-web. The lights go dark, then flicker back on. One big and one small spot of wet are growing on the carpet: the smelly tank water that poured against the wall over the socket, and the ammonia that grows out of a plastic bottle. Daddy's coming toward Jamie. Aw . . . now Jamie . . . Lights off again, then on. Octo's white on the orange carpet with all his legs coiled tight to him, polka-dot suckers exposed. Jamie, c'mon . . . back to your room . . . The socket sparks and the lights go off except the hall light. Jamie's mind is crying like a baby and his body is flying into a Fit of Rage.

Daddy grabs his arms and holds him down. Easy Jamie! Settle down!

Ma, in her nightgown, rushes in. Ron! What's going on? she asked. She clutches Jamie from behind and he elbows her, but she holds on. Shhhh, she whispers into his ear.

Between Ma and Daddy, Jamie can't move.

What did you do Ron? asks Ma.

What do you think? he asks. Shoulda done it long ago.

How can you say that?

They think Jamie's too frantic to hear, but he's taking it all in.

Let me go! he says again and again, first screaming, then his voice cracks into a whimper. Please, let me go.

They let him struggle away.

Nancy! yells Daddy, Go back to bed! Nancy, who was standing in the doorway in her nightgown, runs off.

Jamie picks up Octo. His long legs drop limp, almost to the floor. Where are you taking that? asks Daddy. Jamie, sobbing, carries Octo down the hall. Ma follows him to the bathroom and watches him put Octo in the tub and start filling it, adding sea salt bit by bit

Now Jamie, what are you doin? asks Daddy from the doorway.

He might live! wails Jamie.

Jamie, your pet's dead. And it's not just me that killed it either.

Go away! screams Jamie. I hate you! This is the worst thing that ever happened and you did it!

Don't you talk to me like that, kid.

Daddy steps forward, but Ma stands to stop him. Ron, don't. Just leave him alone.

What, has this place gone nuts, that a kid can talk that way to his dad?

Go away! screams Jamie.

Ron, go. I'll take care of this.

You two are nuts. Ya gonna bring that thing back to life? The thing is dead. And it's happier that way I'm sure.

No he's not, says Jamie. He might live if we keep him in here. We can take him to the ocean and he'll get better.

Take him to the ocean? Daddy laughed. But Ma was already saying, Honey, it's all right. We can take him to the ocean.

What did you say, Judith?

Go, Ron! she yelled.

Nuh-uh, this is crazy. This isn't right. You think a kid could talk to his dad that way when I was a boy? My Pop woulda smacked me upside the head. None of this coulda happened. This is all so fuckin nuts! An octopus livin in my fuckin living room, stinking up the place, and Jamie thinks it's the most important thing on earth. It's all that matters, right? Even though everyone else hates it and the girls are scared to death of it, right? Now Jamie runs the place. We gotta pay good money to feed the ugly thing, so Jamie don't get upset. Fuckin *nuts!* And if it decides to take a stroll around the apartment while we're at work, no problem! Jamie's in charge now and the octopus can do what it likes.

How did you know that Octo got out? cries Jamie.

Elsie. How else?

Ron!

Jamie's head drops and he doesn't move or say anything for a moment. Daddy clenches and unclenches his fists. Then Jamie says in a small voice, so they know he means it, I never want her to come here again.

Oh Honey, says Ma and puts her arms around him.

I don't want her anymore. I don't want any more care providers.

See? says Daddy. Thinks he runs things now.

Judith waves him away.

Jamie turns his back to Daddy and looks down into the tub.

Don't worry, Jamie, says Ma as she turns off the water. Tomorrow morning we'll take him to the ocean and let him go. He'll be okay.

Daddy stomps down the hall yelling something, but no one's listening now.

Jamie puts the bucket on the floor of the back seat, gets in, and braces it between his knees. Nancy sits in the back too, and Jacob's in his seat between them. Rebecca's in front with Ma.

While Jamie was putting Octo into the bucket, Ma had woken up Nancy and Rebecca and got them excited to go on rides at Coney Island. Jamie knows it's just because Daddy's grumbling and needs to be left alone.

They drive. The avenues are like the alphabet—M, N, O, P—leading to the ocean. They pass housing developments, nice neighborhoods with lawns, Jewish men with hats and beards.

Octo looks smaller, sort of deflated. The water is foggy with bits of brown flesh.

Suddenly the signs aren't in English anymore. Nancy asks what kind of writing it is and Ma says it's Russian and it means we're almost there.

Ma parks and they get out of the car. She puts Jacob in the stroller, and they and walk across the lot. The bucket is heavy so Jamie has to walk slow, squinting in the bright sun, but he doesn't want Ma to help him. They walk down a narrow alley between two old brick apartment buildings the color of sand. They climb stairs to the boardwalk. Rebecca helps Ma with the stroller. Old people sunning on benches open their eyes just a little to watch them cross the boardwalk. The sky is perfectly blue and steam is rising from the sand into the hot morning. The stroller won't go onto the sand, so they all wait on the bottom step while Jamie walks across the beach. Nancy wants to go, too, but Ma says to hush, let Jamie do it alone.

It's hard to walk on the soft sand. Jamie staggers across the beach and climbs onto a jetty made of big rocks extending out into the ocean. He hugs the bucket to his chest. It smells bad, but then ocean air gusts the smell away. Jamie hobbles from stone to stone down the jetty, careful not to slip.

About halfway down, he stops. The water looks deep, with sand churning up from the bottom. He puts the bucket down on a flat stone and sits down beside it. A big wave comes and soaks his foot. The water is freezing cold. Much colder than Octo's tank.

But it's okay, because Jamie knows that Octo is really dead. Daddy killed him. Slowly, he tips the bucket. Water trickles, then pours out, then Octo slides out like a lump of trash. He plunges into the water and sinks out of sight. Bye, Octo, says Jamie.

He imagines Octo coming back to life down there in the dark. Filling back up like a balloon, spreading his legs and crawling to deeper water. He imagines it, but his heart isn't in it. He's just telling himself a story, like Ma and Daddy do, to settle him down.

He leaves the bucket there because he doesn't need it anymore, and returns to the others.

They all walk down the boardwalk toward the amusement park. They stop at an open air restaurant for fried egg sandwiches and tater tots, and sit on a bench watching the ocean while they eat. Nancy and Rebecca are talking about the rides, but Jamie doesn't listen.

People are jabbing umbrellas into the sand and setting up lawn chairs. Two black women in bathing suits wade in the water up to their knees. They laugh and shift from foot to foot, hugging their arms to their chests.

When they're done eating, Ma gathers the trash and says, Well kids, ready for the rides?

Nancy and Rebecca ride the bumper cars, but Jamie stays with Ma and Jacob. The park is getting crowded. He feels nervous. He's not used to being around people.

Ma laughs at Rebecca speeding around in her tiny car, and at Nancy butting heads with a teenage boy. Look Jamie, she says.

Yeah, I see.

They go to another ride where Nancy and Rebecca spin around in cars shaped like bumble bees. The cars go up and down and Nancy shrieks and giggles. After they get off Rebecca says that she's bored with these kids' rides. She says she wants to ride the roller coaster. Ma says okay, but it's the last ride cause Jamie's tired.

Jamie can't know this but, down on the beach, Octo has washed up onto the sand. He lays in a brown tangle of legs until a wave comes and rearranges him, taking two legs and setting them like clock hands that say three o'clock. Then another takes him further onto the sand

and turns him upside down so if you looked, you could see the little beak in the middle where all the legs meet.

Two little girls, twin sisters, are digging with pink plastic shovels. One notices Octo.

What is that thing?

I dunno.

They walk over and look down at him.

It's like a sea animal or something. *¡Mira Mama!* she calls to their mother.

¿Mama, qué es esto? asks her sister. She takes her plastic shovel and gives Octo a shy prod.

Their mother, sitting in a lawn chair, lifts her sunglasses. *¡No lo toques, Mija!* she yells.

Ew, says the first girl. That thing is so gross.

But what is it?

I dunno.

¡No lo toques! calls their mother.

There are two signs at the roller coaster: One has an arrow and says YOU MUST BE THIS TALL TO RIDE THE CYCLONE, the other says NO SINGLE RIDERS.

Oh no! whines Rebecca. Nancy's too little, and I can't go on by myself. She looks up at Ma.

Don't look at me, laughs Ma. I've got Jacob.

Rebecca turns to Jamie. Jamie, will you go with me?

Jamie kicks at the dirt.

It'll be fun, Jamie. Please? Otherwise I can't go at all.

Jamie is silent. He doesn't want to go.

And I *really* want to go, says Rebecca

All right, he says finally.

They walk between the rails and give the man their tickets. There are only four other people riding. They climb into the middle car, the man locks down the guard rail, and the cars begin ticking slowly forward.

Thanks, Jamie.

Jamie doesn't respond.

Look, I feel really bad. I'm sorry I fought with you and stuff. I'm sorry I scratched you . . . And I didn't mean it when I said I hated you. I was just mad.

The car lurches into an incline.

Jamie says nothing. He isn't mad at her, and wishes she'd just leave him alone. He watches the blue sky as they climb up and up.

And I'm sorry your pet's dead. I really am. I'm sorry about everything. Jamie? Come on. Please say you forgive me.

But suddenly they're roaring down. Their hearts leap into their throats and they both scream. Rebecca's scream has a laugh in it, but Jamie's is pure terror, like he's facing death. He grabs Rebecca's arm tight and doesn't let go the whole ride.

Intercessor

Greg Miller

He prayed for weeks, till praying grew routine.
He prayed for healing, and his prayers' keen
Insistence brought him sometimes to his knees
As in his mind's eye, images, like bees
From the shook hive, flew. Whom had prayer healed,
Protected? Whom could he, unshielded, shield?
But still he felt compelled: he held to hope
Though when it slipped, it burned him like a rope.
He would do better. He had better sense
Than to be cast aside with no defense.
He sought out Jesus, thinking that he could
Take up the matter: what he got was blood,
Lulled bees, an empty tomb, grape hyacinths,
As walking through the borough's labyrinths,
Holding his sister, thankless healing light
Together in his head, he fought to fight.

OPEN CITY

> Certain paintings by Klimt bring home to me with such immediacy the horrors of the child carrying and birthing labors imposed on the human species that I find myself close to vomiting. This may seem to be in contradiction to the choice of my artistic subjects, for it is true that I carve almost exclusively the Madonna.
> (Rezzori, page 199)

Icepaper #3

Adam Cvijanovic

OPEN CITY

**A man can't fight everything
that comes through the door,
I said to Death.**
      (Shapiro, page 185)

Neck, 17.5"

Siobhan Reagan

AMSTERDAM AGAIN. THE CITY OPENED ITSELF TO HER UNDER A phlegmatic sky. The canals gave off a gamy resinous smell. In her room at the Radisson, Rose peeled off her boots and socks and climbed fully clothed under the cotton quilt on the queen-sized bed. She was shivering. She got up almost immediately to close the heavy drapery more fully against the weak afternoon light. In bed, she closed her eyes against the room, its generic rattan furniture—she had gotten one of the "Indonesian" rooms again, they were less sumptuous than the "Art Deco" or "Olde Scandinavian" styles the hotel also boasted. There was a moment of familiar resistance to the new surroundings, the sense that the room was somehow against her, until she felt her muscles relax and she fell asleep.

    Rose DeWolf is thirty-four years old and she sleeps peacefully in her generic room in the familiar city. She has flown nonstop from New York to Amsterdam without taking—it might even be said she flouted—the usual precautions for flying. There would be no extra moisturizer slathered on hands and throat, no purse-sized spritzer of Evian to freshen up during the flight, no particular avoidance of salty foods, alcohol, or caffeine while in the air. Upon reaching Schiphol airport—graced with a bank of sunflowers at the International-arrivals gate—Rose, bless her heart, immediately lit up a cigarette. Under the cotton quilt she wears an oversized cashmere turtleneck over a man's white Brooks Brothers oxford shirt and a pair of tight fitting black pants. She wears panties bought from a Rite Aid in New

York City, three to a pack, and a white, ever-so-slightly grimy Calvin Klein bra. She has had a manicure recently, but not so recently that the nails of her rather square and practical right hand are not beginning to show signs of wear; the right cuticle of her thumb, for example, is hard, scaly, and bloody from where Rose has chewed it. Rose has brown hair which she wears long and light eyes of an indefinable gray-blue. She is not prone to acne but rather to dry skin, which peels frequently, giving Rose a rather battered look around the nose and mouth. All in all, she is attractive, our Rose, tall and lean, capable still of turning heads when she comes into a room, when she feels good, when she feels like that might be something she'd like to do.

In her sleep, Rose turns to her right side. Her hands creep between her thighs and she clasps them together there—the damaged cuticle of the right hand, the ringless ring finger of the left. Tucking herself into her own corpus this way, Rose sleeps.

Rose's dreaming is a counterpoint to a discovery she has made recently, or thinks she has made recently, which is that she has somehow crossed an indefinable line in her adulthood. She might also call it her "womanhood," but, in her caustic and self-deprecating way, Rose shies away from such a cloying construction. She prides herself, after all, on being beyond the traditional definitions of womanliness. (She is aware, for example, that she is attractive, but resists admitting to it for fear of "capitalizing" on it too much.) Still, the knotty tangle she faces in her long and arduous dream of arriving at an airport, only to discover that she has left her bags at a faraway and nondescript lounge, speaks of Rose's creeping, and perhaps superstitious belief that she has arrived on the other side of a barrier of sorts. She has moved, she believes, from a position of hopefulness about her adult life as a flexible, single career woman, into a position of doubt.

When she wakes, Rose spends several private minutes reviewing her journey and finally picks up the bedside phone. She dials a familiar number and speaks in her halting but well-inflected Dutch to the party on the other end. Forty minutes later Rose emerges from the Radisson onto Rusland, a cobbled street that borders the red-light district. It is dark now, cyclists are returning home to their canal-side flats or trendy houseboat-shares, their bike bells giving off a faint, inadvertent chime as they traverse the bumpy street. Outside the Radisson, a couple of Mercedes cabs wait to pick up passengers. Rose navigates towards the red-light district. She is going to have a massage.

She is lying facedown on the massage table. She can feel her own breasts pushed up hard against her torso in the cotton robe they have given her. She lies under a white sheet waiting for the arrival of her masseuse, a Surinam woman named Jo Jo. Jo Jo's first assault on Rose's back is a pleasure that Rose remembers as a gift of sorts. There is Jo Jo's initial deep push into the center of her upper back, flattening and (momentarily) realigning the muscle and cartilage into a perfect symmetry of flatness.

Jo Jo moves from Rose's back to Rose's feet, and here she lavishes long stroking rubs. Rose's pedicure has remained intact since she left New York. Manicures from the nails sweatshop she frequents on Seventh Avenue seem to disintegrate more quickly. Rose makes a mental note of the fact that it is Asian women who provide her with the necessary upkeep of life: the manicure, pedicure, waxing, and massage that keep her sane. She hopes that Jo Jo notices the care that has been lavished on her toes and feet by an equally anonymous Asian woman. Rose pays cash for everything and she gives Jo Jo a big tip after changing in the massage parlor's dressing room. On a shelf below a big mirror are toiletries familiar to Rose: Dennen and Johnson's Baby Powder and Vitalis. She remembers that she has heard that this massage parlor doubles as a brothel and the toiletries only seem to confirm this. How strange, she thinks, to be massaged like a man in a man's place. Still, the masseuses who loll on sofas in the handkerchief-sized reception area give no indication that Rose is out of place there, and she pays her bill feeling that she has gotten away with something.

Rose walks back along one of the canals, feeling as though her circulation is finally working again after the massage and noticing the late night Amsterdam life as it plays out around her. In the windows she passes are women lit in ultra-violet light which emphasizes the lingerie they wear—some in panties and bras, some in merry-widow-type negligees—all appear unnaturally dark and exotic in the contrast. Some move slowly and sensuously, others sit prosaically in chairs against backdrops of red drape shaving their legs, eating from cartons of take-out food, doing their nails, stroking on mascara or lipgloss. There are Asian women and black women and white women. Rose tries to imagine how they came here, wonders about the pay and hours. They are so far beyond her, she knows. They observe the clusters of thick-necked tourists who move beneath them on the street—implacable, silent, caged, and yet superior for their confinement. Rose watches a man as he enters a ground-level bordello, watches as the woman takes his hand in a friendly way, acknowledges the man's nervousness with a giggle, and motions him to the back of her shop.

Rose makes good money as a consultant and travels, which her friends envy. She gives them nuggets of impersonal yet evocative scenarios—the renovated castle in Scotland, autumn in Stockholm, the spa she stayed at in Frankfurt. Still, there is something clinical and sad about her life on the road, Rose thinks. She does not tell her friends, for example, about the pleasure she gets from drinking alone in the bars of the various upscale hotels in which she stays, does not tell them about the vibrator she smuggles with her into Europe and used, one week, on the floor of her hotel room because the international-adapter cord did not reach to the bed. Does not describe for them how her fantasies become merely generically erotic while she's away; that she's an international call girl, that she's a maid called into the room of a man she doesn't know, that she's seducing the attractive German husband and wife she met at breakfast. Her fantasies when she travels for work take on the sameness of the seminar rooms she works out of and the hotel restaurants she eats in.

Rose stops to drop a gilder in a paper cup being proffered by a blonde woman about her own age off Herengracht. The woman's name is Maisie, she is an expatriate failure, a woman who came to Amsterdam to make art and instead fell in with a crew of Indonesian hustlers. She too is thirty-four, with pale blonde hair, light eyes, and a sweet, dimpling smile. She is dressed badly, except for a pair of green Miu Miu shoes which Rose naïvely admires. At this, Maisie stands up from where she has been sitting—on a bench not too far from the stench of an open-air pissoir, of the kind that punctuate the red-light district—and offers to take Rose to see a friend of hers—someone who will show her a "good time." Rose declines, sensibly; she is, after all, here on business, but Maisie is persistent and persuasive. Rose marvels that she is being led away from her familiar trajectory and into the heart of something she doesn't know, is not sure she even cares to know.

Maisie takes Rose to an apartment building just off Central

Station. They climb a flight of carpeted stairs to a landing—Rose notices a smell of fish and garlic cooking—and Maisie knocks on the door of an apartment. The door is opened by a young man, Asian and black, Rose thinks because of his eyes and his dreads. When they enter, there is room full of people smoking marijuana. The smoke crosses the threshold in great billowing waves, it reminds Rose of parties in college which were marked by a certain desperation to imitate nightlife in Goa or Thailand. Maisie leaves Rose with Basey and moves to the bathroom where there are one or two girls waiting. When she gets there she snorts a small amount of heroin she has been keeping. She looks in the mirror after and her face is the same, she thinks, maybe a little gaunt, or a little puffy? Around the eyes? She's not sure but she smiles a dimpled smile at the mirror.

Meanwhile, Rose furiously calculates the time she has left in which to get fucked-up with Basey (the beautiful Asian-African) and the time left before she needs to make a showing with her teammates from work. They are leading an executive seminar called "Benchmarking: Delivering With Results." She figures that she has at least sixteen hours before she needs to be completely sober and accordingly takes deep hits off a bong offered by Basey. The pot leaves her weak and oxygenated. She looks around and sees the room for the first time: A Jimi Hendrix tapestry hangs from one wall, a small harvest of pot plants growing under ultraviolet bulbs, another giant bong in the corner, and sitting around a low table are five people Rose can only describe as in their early twenties. The girls are wearing satin jeans and navel-baring tops, the boys have self-conscious goatees and heavy, droopy pants. "Get me out of here," some part of Rose's consciousness screams while her body begins to deaden and sink into the futon sofa where she sits. She watches as Basey reaches behind one of the girls at the table to fondle her breasts beneath her halter top. Rose thinks of her own breasts, her own body, so far protected from such intimacy, protected from such excitement. Basey comes over to her and she tries to engage him in a discussion about the Euro. He gives her an indulgent (pitying?) look and moves back to the table where he makes a place for himself among the other smokers. Rose alone remains upright and sitting on the futon. Maisie is nowhere to be seen. She has actually slunk into a bedroom to make a call which she cannot seem to make. She sits near the phone, her head hanging in a long nod.

"What do you do?" Rose is asking Helene of the halter top.

"I read people," Helene answers and giggles, looking at Basey.

"What do you mean?" Rose asks. "Like a palm reader?"

"Sort of," the girl answers, looking away suddenly shy. "I have whaddyacallit—the sixth sense, I can read a person like a book."

What kind of book? Rose wonders. Sidney Sheldon or Tolstoy? Graham Greene or Dr. Suess?

"Like take you for example," the girl, Helene is saying. "I can read you. It wouldn't be perfect, but I could read you, I could tell you something about yourself that's true but that you hide. Like something you don't want others to know."

"Oh YEAH?" Rose says, too harshly, too American-skeptical, she knows, but she can't help herself.

"Yeah," says the girl. "I can tell you what you did the last time you were in Amsterdam. I can tell you about the apartment where you live; I can tell you about your parents and where you grew up.

"You're alone a lot," Helene continues, as though she hasn't noticed Rose's silence and the overarching silence in the room—the boys and girls around the bong have stopped laughing and telling anecdotes, even the stereo sounds softer, although no one has gotten up to turn the volume down. "And sometimes you like it. You're the kind of person who doesn't like to ask for things from other people. *You'd prefer to go it alone.*" Rose has to smile at the sweet formal way that English comes from this Dutch girl's mouth. You'd prefer to go it alone. "But you have a few friends that you'd do anything for," Helene says. She pauses to take a deep drag from a spliff that's being passed around.

"On the other hand," Helene says, exhaling in the direction of Basey, who now has the spliff between two elegant fingers, "You're selfish too. You like to do things by yourself and for yourself. You're the type of person who'd sometimes rather get drunk alone at home than go out with friends you think are beneath you, socially or intellectually. And," Helene pauses, as though gathering steam, "you like to think of yourself as on the cutting edge—or at least on the edge. You pride yourself on being experimental. That's why you're here right now, isn't it?"

Helene looks at Rose candidly with beautiful deep-set blue eyes.

"Okay," Rose says, "But I bet you can't tell me about my apartment."

Walking back through Dam Square, Rose observes the carnival that has been set up there—observes the way that the big Ferris wheel across from the Hotel Krasnopolsky clasps the early morning light and catches the overcast dawn in its spokes and frets, notices the way that it stands apart from the scenery around it: the big white national monument to the Second World War, the Dutch stock exchange and the department store on the corner.

Rose is not thinking about Basey as she crawls again into her bed at the Radisson, but about the man who owned the white oxford shirt that she is wearing. She is thinking about him pulling open the fold-out couch in her apartment and thinking about the way he said "check" as he moved the coffee table, and she is feeling a squeamish pleasure about him and the way that they prepared the room for sex. Or prepared the room for lying together, she can't remember if they had sex that night or not.

But lying in the "Indonesian" room, Rose thinks of Helene and what she said and knows that it is true. She is selfish, she is alone, a lot. She has five hours before she has to meet her colleagues in the hotel bar for a pre-seminar meeting. Rose suppresses a small spiral of panic at the thought of conducting "Delivering With Results" the following day. She is alone, it's true. The man with the oxford shirt didn't work out, like several before him and, probably, Rose thinks, many after him. He resented her traveling and, she thinks, misjudged its glamour.

Rose DeWolf, thirty-four years old, pulls her amulet—a stuffed monkey from a department store in Antwerp—close to her and begins to try to sleep. She feels first the room's animosity towards her, a stranger, and then, as her muscles relax, she sleeps.

**Let him unclog the kitchen drain,
put the children to bed
if he can remember their names**
(Winer, page 141)

My Cocaine Museum

Michael Taussig

Right from the start the great collector is struck by the confusion, by the scatter, in which the things of the world are found.
—Walter Benjamin, "The Collector," *The Arcades Project*

1.

LOOKING AHEAD THROUGH THE NEVER-ENDING RAIN AND shadow of the forest, with the roar of the river on our left, we made out the clatter of machinery and a rusty iron structure like a gigantic funnel, the height of a two-story building located in a deep basin the size of a football field excavated next to bank. It was the *canelón*, the sluice, into which the hillside on the other side of the river was disappearing as so much rock and rubble to be filched for gold. At its base like a yellow centipede crawled a tractor-trailer on its countless tires. The land was cleft by landslides into which trees and surface vegetation disappeared leaving nothing but gray soil, cracked and oozing, insides of a bleeding carcass, at which two bulldozers were picking. A pipeline vomited orange water into the cascade spilling over the turmoil of boulders that had once been a purposeful river. Awkwardly balancing on the rubble, a *mestizo* man with a black rubber cape stood guard with a shotgun. Some children and barely clad women who had been panning for gold at the edges of this mountain of rubble and sliding mud, walked calmly in front of the trailer, balancing their wooden pans upside down on their heads as umbrellas. Not that they seemed to care much about the rain. It seemed like a cute, even comic, act amid this grotesque drama, those black silhouettes against the warm sheets of rain, the gray sky and the leaden air. We'd returned to the beginning and end of time when the planet was formed from molten chaos and was now disappearing into it. "What is your mission? What is your mission?" people ask us as we struggle through the mud to the village.

2.

The women bend from the waist and like magic get the batea to make this swirling movement so that the center spins out the stones. Every so often they dip the edge into the river so more water spills in with every swirl. After a minute or so there remains a black sand fine as soot in which they look for specks of gold. It is an astonishingly beautiful movement. I try my hand at it and the gravelly water sloshes around and I lose all of it. When the women stoop, the bodies bend into the running water through the medium of this spinning wooden disc, the batea, which is about two feet across and saucer-shaped. The trick is to get the rotating action working in harmony with the up-and-down action just at the level of the water in the stream so that as the non-gold bearing material is ejected by centrifugal force, a little water is allowed to spill in by a centripetal force. What sort of machine could do that? Each woman works on her own, occasionally in groups of two. They take their washing with them, often some small kids, and the pace is leisurely. Even tiny kids work the batea, almost as big as themselves. On an average day they earn the peso equivalent of almost two dollars this way, working from early morning to mid-afternoon. I am surprised the women can tell me on repeated occasions this same figure. It seems so routine. I thought panning for gold would be prone to chance and the excitement thereof. Perhaps they work to that figure and then call it quits for the day. Or perhaps what they get varies greatly day to day but nobody wants the others to know if they score big. Later I learn how sensitive people here are to envy and inequality, to sorcery as payback, and the devil as the master of a miner's fate. For their work does share something with hunters and gamblers, following a trace, subject to chance. What sort of work is this? The hunt as work is very primitive, said Walter Benjamin, and the life-long experience of the person who has to attend to the trace results only remotely from work, if at all. Such experience, he went on to say, has no sequence and no system. It is a product of chance and exhibits the interminability of the idler, prototypical of study.1 It was the configuration of knowledge as experience that caught his eye, the mix of long-term experience with immediate, shock-like, stimulus—the glitter of gold at the bottom of the batea—reacting back on that life of experience that comes to the adult who started this hunting and gambling, gambolling as a five year old by the edge of the stream, working alongside its mother.

9.

My first sight of the Russian miners was of blond shirtless men staggering into the dusk along the uneven cobblestones of the one street that is Santa María, clutching at bottles of rum that in those gigantic hands seemed more like toys. It was unnerving for you rarely see shirtless men in other parts of Colombia, let alone blond ones on the Pacific Coast, and their lurching desperation made them stand out like clowns on a stage. And these chain-smoking men, more often drunk than not, were desperate. They would laugh and weep in quick succession, their Colombian translator told me, and often fight. For apart from the rigors of the climate and the remoteness of the location, they had not been paid, so it was said, either in pesos or in rubles, much less in the precious dollars they had been promised. They were prisoners no less than those in Gorgona had been, stuck to hell up an isolated river in the Colombian jungle. There were supposed to be one hundred of them, according to a submission to the circuit court in Guapi (and seventy four Colombian employees as well). They could barely muster a word in Spanish. *"Santa María! No problema! Santa María! No problema!"* That was about it. Except for the word *contrato*. The locals treated them with scant respect. The Russians slunk in and out of the village back to their camp by the airstrip. When asked what most impressed them about Colombia, one responded with wide open eyes, "The goods in Buenaventura!" The main port on the Pacific Coast, Buenaventura bakes in a muddy estuary of cheap shoes, cheap Scotch, and cheap lives. The Russians pass around my son's red flashlight. It passes from hand to hand in its smooth perfection. I am the first white man handing out beads, cloth, and guns to these semi-naked barbarians living off hope and fearing

---

[1] Walter Benjamin, "Idleness," Convolute M in *The Arcades Project* (Cambridge: Harvard University Press), pp. 801-02.

strange gods (names supplied on request). I shall write a book about their cruel customs and become famous. They buy a bottle of rum and fill seven glasses. We stand up and drink. They are not miners, I say to myself. They are earth-movers. We brace ourselves.

10.

The village lies at the headwaters of the River Timbiquí where the river runs fast and hard down the Andes over sheets of rapids bordered by rain forest to empty out through mangrove swamps into the Pacific Ocean directly across from the small island of Gorgona that between 1960 and 1985 was Colombia's highest security prison. It is in this sort of upriver country, alerted by the Indians as to abundant surface deposits of gold, that the Spaniards founded mining settlements based on African slaves in the eighteenth century. After abolition in 1851, the ex-slaves stayed on mining for themselves and refusing to work for their previous owners for a wage. White men had always feared for their lives on the Pacific Coast anyway, what with the massive rainfall, highest in the Americas and possibly the world, the terrible heat and humidity, and what nineteenth century geographers called "the miasmatic exhalation" of the four hundred miles of mangrove swamps. The village lies where the gold is, way upriver from the swamp. It is called Santa María (pop. 2,500) and I first visited it in 1971 and then again in 1976. At the town of Guapi, when I returned in 1992, I had been warned that drug money from the interior city of Pereira (names supplied on request), had contracted a Russian outfit to mine the jungle along the banks of Santa María, and that I should be prepared, they said with knowing smiles, for drastic changes. For times now were different. All of Colombia was changing, most especially the Coast, now thrown open to world markets by state invitation officially labeled as the *apertura* or "opening," cosmic in promise, like the mythic riches of the Amazon. For despite, if not because of appearances to the contrary you could, with the assurance of *apertura*, peer through the haze of humidity, mud, and malaria, and discern, so it was said, and the language was palpable, the dazzling wealth in gold, copper, uranium, platinum, fish, shrimp, amazing freshwater shrimp too, flown to the restaurants of Paris, so I was told, hardwoods, the world's finest, Chachajo, Mulato, Narde, Pava, Amarillo, Guyacan, Guamo, Guasimo, Caymitillo, Roble, Soaje, Anime, Jeli,

Chaciro, Chanul, Justa Razon, Pantano, Sande, and stands of softer wood like Higua Negra, Galsa, Higua Para, Nasde and soft woods such as the giant Nato, Cuángare, Sajo, Cedro, and Tangare, mangrove for railway ties, mangrove bark for tanning, hearts of palm . . . not to mention even more alluring fantasies such as the alleged markets of the Pacific Rim and even a new canal to rival what the gringos built in Panamá, with an overhead railway above the forest, to be constructed by the Koreans . . . and, of course, Biological Diversity and the drama of its imminent demise, of which, more later.

11.

When we had embarked at Guapi for the Timbiquí River, my new schoolteacher friend said "The Russians put it about they are looking for gold, but it's uranium they're after! Gold is the least valuable thing they mine! They are tearing the wealth from the ground. In ten years they'll take out as much as the four hundred years since the Spanish Conquest!" The Russians create quite a stir. Downriver from Santa María at the regional capital of Santa Barbara where the company is headquartered, people automatically assumed we were Russians too. Some people are taking Russian classes from the Colombian interpreter, and the one general store of any size in Santa Barbara is well stocked in vodka, at least double the price of Colombian rum. Rumor has it that the owner, Mauro, is a partner in the mine too, making money hand over fist. Russian managers push past me rudely and go into his office. At Santa María, way upriver, Omar tells me Russians are animals, they eat sun-dried fish without cooking it, they drink like crazy men, and they bulldozed down the statue of Julio Arboleda at San Vincente. Gustavo, the sweetest of men, says they smell awful. Lydia says they are racist. Omar rips them off terribly with his beer prices, even more than he does his friends and neighbors. So do the people who own what I call the "blue bar" where the prostitutes from Buenaventura hung out till the Russians found local girls who charge less. People seem afraid of the Russians yet like the services they provide, such as the electricity generator and the mechanics who fix their pumps for a few beers. (Since the 1960s these pumps have transformed and given a new lease to peasant mining because they allow you to excavate vertically regardless of water levels.) What is strange about this virtual fetishization of the company as "the Russians" is

OPEN CITY

how conveniently people forget that the impetus behind their presence is, more than likely, not only Colombian capital but that the whole deal required careful orchestration by somebody from Santa María with considerable knowledge and expertise concerning the gold there. *"Santa María! No problema!"* One day there will be an explosion here. Then we'll see about eating uncooked fish!

12.

Some other notes about Guapi: calendars with photos of nude blonde women are prolific, especially where outboard motors and chain saws are sold. The day broke humid and heavy under a steel gray sky over a steel gray river. Two women in canoes gliding like phantoms, backs stiff in their portable canoe seats, little armchairs, elaborately carved like the balconies on the second floor of the houses you find all over the coast.

13.

I ask a friend what happens to the gold he mines and sells. He says it goes to the Banco de la República in Bogotá which sells it to other countries. "What happens to it then?" "I don't really know. They put it in museums . . ." His speech fades. Lydia shrugs at this question, too. It's for jewelry, she thinks. And for money. People sell it for money. It goes to the Banco de la República and they get money for it . . . In a burst of self-righteousness I ask myself how come the world famous Gold Museum of the Banco de la República in Bogotá has nothing, absolutely nothing, about African slavery, or about the lives of these gold-miners whose ancestors were bought as slaves to mine the gold that was for centuries the basis of the colony—*just as cocaine is today?* As the fetish that has so long underpinned the value of value, gold absorbs history into its shimmering self and replaces it with a timeless prehistory of intriguing pre-Colombian artifacts locked in glass display cases in the bank's elegant building downtown Bogotá. And while we're on the subject, shouldn't the Banco de la República be creating a Cocaine Museum alongside its famous Gold Museum now that cocaine is so important economically and determines the country's political future, if there is a future? Cocaine not only has a good deal of the prehistoric too, changing temporalities and evoking strange bodily rhythms out of time, but its production and distribution are no less based on violence and coercion than was African slavery in the New World. And like cocaine today, gold production in Colombia was subject to intense legal control (by the Spanish crown) and subterfuge by mine owners in order to evade that control. So what would a Cocaine Museum look like? What would you put in it? It is so tempting, so almost within grasp, this imaginary project whose time has now come. So necessary too. Like a game for children, museums should exist to see if we have grasped the lesson by finding a way of playing with it. In fact, thinking through what should go into such a museum would be worth a whole lot more than the finished display. Its main feature as worthy successor to the Gold Museum would be to revel in the display of luxury and crime as the basis of any social worth. And where better to start than right here or with Wall Street brokers and teevee personalities buying their drugs from a Dominican man in a nice suit in the men's room sniffing cocaine while across the East River at Kennedy airport a Chesapeake Bay retriever named Aby, also sniffing for drugs urged on by its U.S. Customs-uniformed mistress, "Go Boy! Go Find it! Good Boy!" as small-statured Colombians draw back in horror at the baggage carousel as their plastic-wrapped oversized suitcases come lumbering into sight and smell—plastic wrapped in Colombia by special businesses that come to your home the day before the flight to seal your baggage against a little slippage. A real American decides enuff is enuff. The dog has gotten out of control, he decides, and tells its handler to back off as the dog jumps up and down slobbering on his chest. "You have your constitutional rights," says the handler. "Here everyone is guilty until smelled innocent," and urges the dog to leap higher. Yet the dog (actually a real live dog that belongs to the Cocaine Museum and doubles up at night as a watchdog) is so high-tech that he is impervious to the smell of the adjacent toilet bowl full of feces and tightly knotted condoms full of cocaine surrounded by pairs of eyes, blown up, showing only the whites of terror as other condoms explode within the stomachs of couriers while realtors in New York City and Singapore shuffle skyscrapers and mansions for favors from the chiefs of police and elected politicians whose task it has been to apply brutal sanctions so as to pay for the War On Drugs so as to maintain sky-high prices for drugs and the expanding prison building industry while keeping the borders between rich and poor areas of the city securely policed. In an adjoining room of the Cocaine Museum next to a photo of a stoic looking Indian woman in traditional garb, eyes averted, seated on the ground with piles of limestone and coca leaves for sale in front of her, there is a large sign that says, "JUST SAY NO!" on the door of William Burroughs's icebox with smiling Nancy Reagan underneath gazing thoughtfully at an automobile with the trunk open and two corpses stuffed inside it with their hands tied tightly behind their backs and neat bullet holes, one each through the right temple and one each through the crown of the head. "Professional job!" exclaim the mourners crowding around the open coffin, holding the neatly dressed children high for a better view.

One of the bodies is Henry Chantre who while doing his military service in the Colombian army used to pick up and transport drugs into Cali for his officers and on discharge got into trafficking himself, a shiny sports utility vehicle now choking the tunnels and bridges leading into New York and favored by Mayor Giuliani, favorite of death squads ever since the Ford Bronco came out, a blonde wife, handsome little children and one day a deal went sour and he was found in the trunk of an abandoned car by the Cauca River, a long way from East River, in one sense. The ripples on the river where black men dive to excavate sand for the drug-driven construction industry in Cali fan out wider and wider. Father Bartolomé de las Casas, sixteenth century savior of Indians in the New World, wrote passionately about the cruelty in making Indians dive for pearls off Margarita in the Caribbean. Nowadays, long after African slavery has been abolished, the slavery that replaced the slavery of Indians, it's considered routine that men would blow their lungs diving for sand, not pearls, and in the ripples of the first ring we discern as if through early morning mist coming off the river the uniformed figures of the guerrilla looking exactly the same as the Colombian army which looks exactly the same as the U.S. Army and all armies from here to eternity collecting the tax from the coca growing peasants forced to pay off their protectors in the cleared fields pressed tight into the *selva* of the Putumayo and Caquetá. Then in the next ring of watery reflections we see the shimmering towers of Cali, poking through the rainbow-hued layers of exhaust-fumes. The city has been transformed by drug money invested in high-rise construction, automobiles, and real estate. To the south of the city, in the next room of our Cocaine

Museum, are the remains of peasant plots like bomb craters, filled with water lilies, in the good flat land from which the earth has been scooped out eight feet deep so as to make bricks and roof tiles for the building boom in the city. This rich black soil, many feet thick, was once the ashes of the volcanoes that floated down onto the lake that was this valley in prehistoric times. Peasants sell it, their birthright, taking advantage of the high prices for raw dirt and because the intense use of chemicals by agri-business has created ecological mayhem and their traditional crops are in ruins. Then the boom stopped and there is no work at all. The music in the museum is sad. The money has been spent. There is no farm anymore. Just a hole with lilies the kids love to swim in. And to tell the truth, for a lot of people even if there was "work" in the city, nobody would want it. Dragging your arse around from one humiliating and massively underpaid job to another 'cause no one will hire you longer than it takes to avoid social security payments. That's all over now, the idea of work work. Now there's more to life. Motorbikes, automatic weapons. But for some reason they are harder and harder to get a hold of. The Cali cartel exists no longer, they say. Not even crime pays anymore and drug dreams by the swamps in the lowest part of the city like Aguablanca where all drains drain and the reeds grow tall through the bellies of stinking rats and toads. Aguablanca. The gangs multiply and the flimsy door is shoved in by the tough guys to steal the teevee and the sneakers off the feet of the sleeping child, the *bazuco* makes you feel so good, your skin ripples and you feel like floating while the police who otherwise never show and the local death-squads hunt down and kill addicts whose bodies are found in gutters and by the sides of streams, twisted front to back as when thrown off the back of the pickup like the jerky movements of the Cali and Medellín cartels on their show horses, *paso fino*, with wide cow-hide leggings dwarfing the clever little horses adroitly curtsying before a huge neon sign, JUST SAY NO, as one is sucked by authentic Indian flute music and the moonlit howls of cocaine sniffing dogs welcoming you to the Gold Museum on the next floor of the Banco de la República.

Something like that.

14.

Gold is what fairy tales can never have enough of because gold has the unique function of being both symbol and reality of value. When Massachusetts sealer Captain Amaso Delano, whose published diary provided Herman Melville with his story, "Benito Cerreno," visited the mint in Lima in 1805 he found himself in a fortress-like building occupying an entire block.[2] The gold ore was wetted and kneaded by blacks treading on it with their feet on a paved brick surface, after which they put mercury on it so as to separate out the gold. Then the metal was heated, becoming as red as blood. So as to get the liquid metal to run from its crucible, the spout had to be touched with a small stick with a piece of cloth around it. When this stick makes contact, a flash will blaze and immediately the metal runs in a small stream not much thicker than a pipe stem. The bars of gold formed are then squeezed flat by rollers until the thickness of a dollar or doubloon, by which time the bars have become sheets four feet long. A powerful press cuts out the exact size and the pieces are then turned edgeways to receive a milled edge. Then comes the weighing. Rarely are the coins too heavy. If they are, they are let through. But if too light, a man selects a tiny pin of precious metal from a box and with a special instrument makes a hole in the coin into which he pushes the pin so as to make the correct weight. The machine which inserted the pin had massive leverage, up to one hundred tons. They were working on thousands of coins when Delano visited, and could pin fifteen a minute, or one every four seconds. The bullion was brought to the mint by private owners, just like people bring corn to a mill. As soon as it was coined, it was taken away by its owners.[3]

15.

I can think of few better ways of making money both more mysterious and everyday than through this meaty description of its making. Here in their minting, gold and silver coins become stark fetishes, material things aglow with a power emanating from deep within. All sense of money as a symbol, of money as the embodiment of societal value, disappears as we become suffused by the mechanical and prac-

---

[2] Charles Olson cites Delano in *Call Me Ishmael* (Baltimore: John Hopkins) p. 117. "[Melville] was a sea frontiersman like the whalers Fanning, Delano and other outriders."

[3] Amasa Delano, *Narrative of Voyages and Travels in the Northern and Southern Hemispheres* [1817] (New York: Praeger), 1970, pp.498-508

tical details of the production of money, including those strange value-added pins. Yet is it not this practicality and this materiality which evokes mystery? In his essay on surrealism, Benjamin counsels the need for a dialectical optic which discerns the mystery in the everyday, no less than the everyday-ness of the mysterious. Surely money, and especially gold coins, qualify as the most surreal of all our objects? It is as if the wonder of materials is freed under capitalism because of the social excision of the social, as Marx interpreted the value of commodities in general, and of money in particular. Gold thus becomes a free agent floating in the ether, the mix of beauty and mystery in money, its power and its evil, is well expressed in its becoming red like blood when heated and liquefied.

16.

In opposition to Newton, beholden to God as the Great Geometer and whose atomistic and mathematical ways of looking at things is certainly congenial to the reifications of gold as money, Goethe wrote a four hundred page book on the theory of colors.[4] This book is filled with mysteries and ingenious experiments that Newton's theory of color as different sized waves of light could not easily encompass. Indeed, Goethe's experiments have been hailed as evidence for a new-fangled "chaos theory." Wiping away breath on glass and then immediately breathing on it once again allows us, he wrote, to see very vivid colors gliding through each other. As the moisture evaporates the colors change their place and at last vanish altogether. Iridescence also appears in soap bubbles and in the froth of chocolate. When first created, bubbles are colorless. Then colored stripes like those in marble paper, begin to appear. This is even easier to see in the bubbles of chocolate froth than in soap bubbles because chocolate bubbles are smaller and the heat provides an impulse towards movement and hence a succession of appearances. As the bubble gets close to bursting we note an attraction of colors towards the highest point of the bubble in which a small circle appears that is yellow in its center while the other colored lines move constantly around this. Slowly this circle enlarges then sinks down and while its yellow center remains, outside it becomes red and soon blue. Sometimes green is produced by the

---

[4] Johann Wolfgang von Goethe, *Theory of Colors*, translated by Charles Lock Eastlake [1840], (Cambridge: MIT) 1970, pp.195 ff.

union of colors at the border. When metals are heated colors rapidly succeed one another. At a certain temperature the metal will be overspread with yellow. As the temperature increases the yellow becomes more intense and passes to red—the red of gold in the Lima smelting house—yet this is difficult to maintain because it hastens to a beautiful bright blue and then a light blue. Goethe (whom I have been quoting and paraphrasing) says at this point that "these colors pass like breath over the plate of steel." Goethe's colorworld is one of movement and sudden change coming from who knows where and into what. It is like magic, like the colored illustrations in children's books and certain forms of abstract expressionism. Walter Benjamin followed this line of thinking in his opposition of color to line. Color was a suffusion unlocking fantasy and taking one into a riotous world, nowhere more so than with the illustrations in childrens' books and the child's love of soap bubbles, not to mention, I might add, their love of chocolate. Even as an adult, Goethe must have held onto childish characteristics. This would account for the ingenuity of his color experiments which convert physics into poetry such that the language of nature and the nature of language become one.

17.

If you hold a sheet of black paper in the sun, Goethe said, "it will be seen to glisten in its minutest points with the most vivid colors." Making color come out of blackness seems miraculous. It is like seeing gold flecks emerge in the black paydirt at the bottom of the spinning *batea* in a woman's strong hands dipping into the stream. William Burroughs is one of the few writers I know who brings color into the picture (along with smell). There is Margaras the dreaded White Cat. The Tracker who, "having no color, he can take all colors ... he moves down windy streets with blown newspapers and shreds of music and silver paper in the wind."[5] And there is also Smoker the black cat named after volcanoes on the floor of the deep oceans. A "creature of the lightless depths" Smoker brought light and color with him as colors pour from tar.[6] Black and White. And Gold. And all those black feet treading gold ore on a paved brick floor followed by a mercury

---

[5] William Burroughs, *The Western Lands* (New York: Viking), pp. 56-7.
[6] Ibid, p. 247.

bath so as to make doubloons and pieces of eight glowing as colors pour from tar.

53.

One thing is a picture, drawn from the imagination. It was another thing to speed around the river and have the universe rip apart with the sound of a compressor and see a navy-blue spaceman, his black face shrouded in glass and his head covered with the helmet of the wet-suit. He goes down in the murky green water. Now and again bubbles come to the surface. He is twelve feet down, they say. The raft is tied to trees on the bank. The current is strong. A hefty man with a slender pole maybe fifteen feet long pokes in a blue metal box from which gushes water and mud pumped up from the river bottom by the *buzo* (diver) below, feeling his way in the dark. The man on the surface uses his pole to dislodge stones that get caught in the outflow which emerges with tremendous force down the three foot wide sluice into which the gold-bearing paydirt is meant to settle. You can't hear yourself think on account of the noise. It upsets your balance. Another man comes with a yellow plastic gasoline container. He pulls out the stick that serves as a plug, sucks on a tube, and empties out the gasoline into the motor supplying air to the man in the dark water below. I wonder how much of the gas fumes go into the air he is breathing down there. What happens if the motor stops for lack of fuel?

54.

The young man opposite where I live in Santa María works as a *buzo*. His wife lives with him, and his girlfriend lives in the house next to me. Sometimes at night he likes to drink *biche* and play music with friends, Ecuadorian music with sad flutes, and *Vallenatos* from the Caribbean coast of Colombia. The stereo has big speakers, and requires a gasoline fueled electric generator which makes a hell of racket. One night they were outside drinking *biche* getting drunk, the music louder and louder, the generator groaning to keep up. Behind the houses, the little river Sese ripples over the stones under the palms and breadfruit trees. By four or five o'clock in the morning, the music and the generator are still going strong when, half sleep under the mosquito net I hear a new sound joining in, the church bells on the hill. The bells keep on much longer than they normally do in the morning. Half an hour goes by and still they ring out. But they sound strangely irregular. Like morse code. Lydia tells me this is because today is the *Día General de Las Animas*, November 2, day after *Todos Los Santos* or All Saints' Day. This is the day for the dead, she explains. If you have had someone die recently, or wish to remember people in your family who died even a long time ago, you pay a boy to go up the hill to the church to pray the Lord's Prayer and ring the bells. This goes on till six o'clock at night. When it stops, she tells me, you keep hearing the bells for a long time inside your head. The bells are rung so as to match the words of the Lord's Prayer. It's a code the kids learn and that's why it sounds irregular, as if the bells are speaking or are meant to be speaking the prayer. It sounds implausible to me. Perhaps a *secreto* is involved. What do I mean? That the bells might "match" the Lord's Prayer, but not by means of a code so much as they give expression to the ground from which all codes emerge. They speak in their own language, we might say, not information nor language as a means, but rather language as a source of experience filling now all space and time all day long jarring and soothing in turns. The Lord's Prayer, what's more. By eight o'clock the music from the *buzo* in front has stopped. With her imperturbable wisdom, Lydia explains it has stopped because the drunks have run out of *biche* and taken a turn ringing the bells to gain a few pesos to buy more.

55.

All day long the bells ring. Ding ding, dong dong, ding . . . dong, ding ding ding . . . wherever you walk, talk, read, look up at the sky or down at the earth or take a shit in the quiet darkness under the house, pat the dog, calm Lydia's baby, eat lunch, this mad sound beside and inside you, ding ding, dong dong, ding . . . dong dong . . . just a small village with basically one wide street of cobblestones and a string of wooden houses either side. The sound becomes an intimate part of you, like your arm, your sweat, or your heart-beat, an elemental part of the universe like the rain, like the river of time's endless flow into the street, through the houses and the mottled cement church up on the hill where the bells are, and beyond all of this, of course, the dead. A comfort. But also unnerving. How close do you want to get? Is it that it never stops? Is it the irregularity? If it was the actual words, it wouldn't seem irregular, would it? And what is it what happens to irregularity when its repeated all day long? I am fifty-eight years old and this bell donging in my ear all day is without a doubt the most sacred event of my life. A crowning performance. My past life stretches out before me like a ribbon. All my friends all over the world since I was a child. They are here too. I write a letter to my friend the other side of the Pacific whom I have known since I was five years old, knowing he never replies.

140.

Yesterday, December 5, 1997, near the Venezuelan border where there is a lot of oil, the Bishop of Tibú, was kidnapped by the E.L.N. (*Ejército Nacional de Liberación*) guerrillas. On the same day in the capital city of Santa Fe de Bogotá, the head of public relations of the president's office was also kidnapped. But by whom? (Note that with the triumph of neo-liberalism we have nevertheless gone back to colonial and religious names, hence the Santa Fe recently restored to the Bogotá.) Also that day the national Department of Security, the D.A.S., often referred to as the secret police, offers a million pesos reward for information leading to the apprehension of Fidel Castaño, the man behind the para-military groups which have been on a wild killing spree in the north of the country, clearing out the guerrillas by massacring peasants. The paras are widely held to be covertly sustained by the armed forces of the state itself, although the real situation may be a good deal worse than that. The para-militaries probably are stronger than the regular army and well able to finance and arm themselves now. The photo supplied by the D.A.S. turns out to be a mistake. It is not of Castaño, leader of the paras, but of the chauffeur of the publisher of a weekly news magazine, *La Semana*. What is more, as announced on television, Castaño's fingerprints cannot be located in the D.A.S. archive. They are lost. He too has been massacred. He too has had body-parts dismembered. He exists without trace. One of the Disappeared. A vacuum for a home. And if the secret police can be infiltrated like this, what of all our other secrets? Truly this is worse than dictatorship where terror channels the mute-absurd.

63.

Surveying the rivers of the Pacific coast that run down the western slopes of the cordillera (like the Timbiquí river), two mining engineers, Henry Granger and Edward Treville, were astonished towards the end of the nineteenth century at the great bodies of gravel they saw, up to millions of cubic yards, they said, which had been moved entirely by hand. They assumed that most of this had been done by slaves, sometimes with the aid of water pressure provided by canals over a league in length or by small dams built to catch rainwater.[7] The coast abounds in powerful natural forces. What the rivers don't erase, the forest will cover in a year or so. But here we have a miraculous glimpse into the shaping of nature by the human hand, a monument to man's domination over nature through his domination over others.

64.

A strong woman covered with mud ordering a bunch of kids carrying buckets of mud to the edge of the hillside late afternoon. Freshly cut orange logs stacked upright by the gaping entrance of the mine they are opening, dense forest all around, the river Little Sese far below. She says mini-dredges or *dragetas* came here first with a John Kenner, it sounds like, from the United States. He traveled by helicopter, using the air strip built by the Russians, and started mining in the river Sese, tributary of the Timbiquí, at San Vincente where the legendary slave owner, Julio Arboleda was born, just below Santa María, The pilot's name was Omar. It was Gustavo who showed John Kenner where the gold was likely to be. The same Gustavo who saunters off so leisurely every day to pan a little gold, the only man in the village to do so. They stayed a year and found no gold, she says. We are standing high on a hillside in the forest with this army of children burrowing into the great black mouth of a reawakened mine. It is hard to imagine a world of helicopters but knowing the pilot's first name helps.

65.

"Surveying the rivers of the Pacific coast that run down the western slopes of the cordillera (such as the Timbiquí River), Granger and

---

[7] Henry G. Granger and Edward B. Treville, "Mining Districts of Colombia," pp. 33-87, *Transactions of the American Institute of Mining Engineers*, vol. 28, February 1898-October 1898, pp. 79,83. Note several pointed critiques of this article in the same volume.

Treville were astonished at the great bodies of gravel they saw, up to millions of cubic yards, they said, which had been moved entirely by hand." I am repeating myself because I want to ask, What is it about the past that makes me want to cite it? Why am I so attached to these millions of cubic yards of gravel? Is it their monumental anti-monumentality? Is it their sprawling silence (which the historian shall shatter in the cause of redeeming the past)? This gets close, but these explanations gesture to something harder to pinpoint and that is the passing of history into nature, a passing so complete that no outsider other than a mining engineer or a geologist would recognize this signal from the slave past. This strikes me as creating something quite different than what is thought of as the romance of ruins such as the crumbling battlement in Europe, or the pathos of the bulldozer left rusting in the tropical forest, vines and snakes happy crawling over their new-found habitat. Ruins are rare in rain forests, anyway, because rain, heat, and insects rot wood, and the vegetation hides anything else within a few years. A pitiless nature triumphs over man's puny artifacts. The point is that decay actually boosts the law of progress which itself acquires natural force through the drama of the ruin. Nature and artifice fuse through a complex rhythm of alienation in which the very decay of the human artifact redeems the triumph of man's technical interventions. Benjamin cites Karl Borinski concerning the baroque cult of the ruin: "The broken pediment, the crumbling columns are supposed to bear witness to the miracle that the sacred edifice has withstood even the most elemental forces of destruction, lightning and earthquake."[8] Nature becomes Progress and vice versa and although the transcendent and religious character of this may be obscured in modernity, the critical role of the ruined fragment of the totality is the same, especially with regards to the passing of history into landscape.

66.

Another way of thinking about a ruin is that it is "unnatural natural." And this is especially so with these immense bodies of gravel. By profession the engineer, such as the persons who pointed out these sprawling bodies of stones in the rain-sodden forest, is a person who straddles the natural and artificial worlds and as allegorist sees writ-

---

[8] Walter Benjamin, *The Origin of German Tragic Drama*, p. 178.

ing in nature in the form of immense gravel deposits that lie across the pages on which nature writes and rewrites its eternal returns. Unnaturally natural is the law of allegory. In this it stands at arm's length from what is often assumed as the law of the symbol which implicates a mute perfection, immaculately fusing nature with culture, the material vehicle of meaning, with meaning itself. The materiality is erased in the meaning, and vice versa. It is an epiphany, a redemption, in the transcendent and theological sense as when in Plato's Symposium, carnal love passes via the body and sheds its material self so as to merge with the nobility of the Idea such that truth and beauty are adored for "their own sakes." By contrast, the allegorical mode of expression is an unresolved dialectic of extremes between form and content in which body and concept wait suspended in the wings like two lovers separated by a chasm with their hands touching now and again. The allegorical mode insistently places the materiality of the form of expression into the form itself such that the resulting meaning is an awkward spread of conflicting possibilities like the gravel deposits sprawling over river banks under exuberant forest cover, in a word, in a paradox, unnaturally natural. Here Eros knows new adventures as the dialectic of human history and nature has been arrested by unimaginable forces of slave-labor for gold in the equatorial rain forest. To break the silence of the past is to trace allegorical modes of writing across the face of a sleeping giant whose awakened memories would stir the earth itself. Millions of cubic yards worth, moved entirely by hand. Into this human history as natural history go miners in search of fossils and gold, prehistoric signs of the Flood when nature convulsed in on itself, mountains fell, the rivers went underground with their newly formed treasure, and what was one day to become the prison-island of Gorgona rose out of the Pacific Ocean, shaking white foam from its tresses.

Untitled

Martin G. Larralde

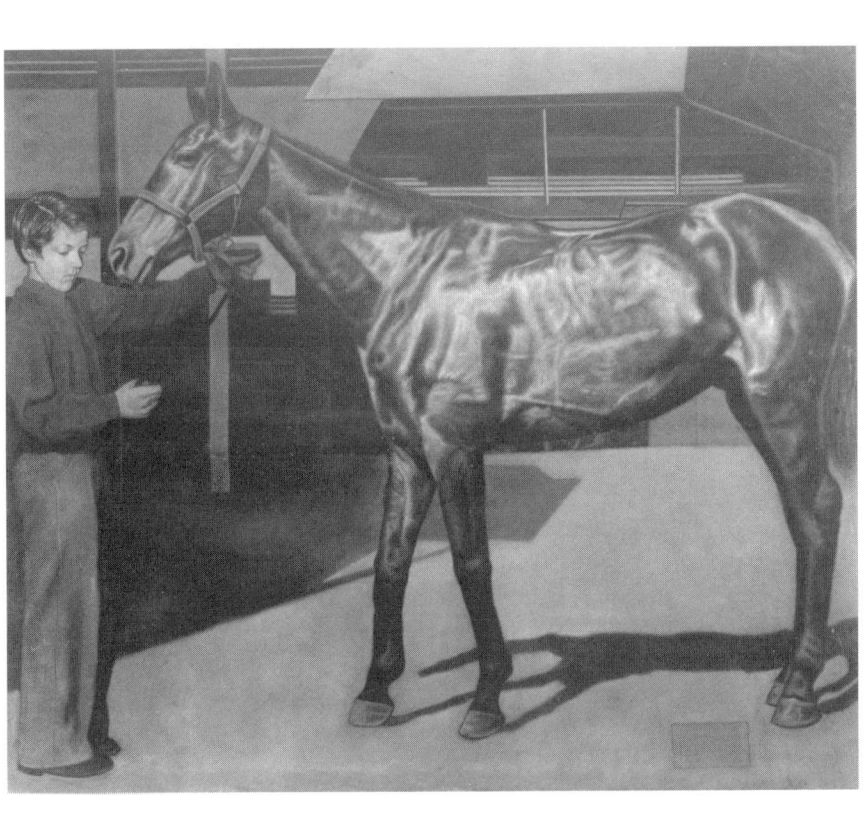

OPEN CITY

Just then the bathroom door crashed open. Joe sailed out in his wheelchair, naked, except for Kellen's blue headband. *Do-lo-reys* . . . he sang out. *Do-lo-reys* . . . Before she could look away, Iris saw his erection, like a long white piano key.

    (Pritchard, page 155)

The Width of the World

Peter Bakowski

I see you,
caught up
in the sculpture
of yourself,

somewhere between

solitude and gossip,
fear and desire,
regret and learning,

perhaps grasping

a pen

the hips of another

or just

the bars of your cage,

sometimes
less than thankful
for
the question marks
crowding
your mind and heart.

OPEN CITY

Are you being brave with your life?

Are you heading toward your needs or your ruin?

Perhaps
only the hands of the clock
will mine
for the answers.

2 A.M.

You lend your restlessness
to the waiting streets.

The moon
has dressed the river
in borrowed light.

Beneath its surface
those who couldn't bear
the cost of wishes,
play
accordions of water.

You linger on the bridge,
till headlights pierce
your brooding,
your envy.

You sit on a park bench,
watch the town hall clock
steal an hour.
At last,
rain scolds you home.

You sit in your room.
Three cigarettes
buy you

Peter Bakowski

the dawn.
A summer ant crawls down
the open window.
You watch it
go out into
the width of the world
with its
vulnerability
and cherished burden.

We Are So Rarely Out of the Line of Fire

Peter Bakowski

A man asleep on the winter pavement
next to his bottle of rum.
A room full of antiques
where the hostess talks about
her third husband.

The moon is in the sky
above
gossip and despair.

Reality
owns more
than
the rain and the lightning,
it toys with
our puppet-strings,
the teetering scales
of give and take.

For some
hope lights the fuse
of choice.
For some
choice
explodes in their face.

Sadness and happiness?

Peter Bakowski

Well,
personally
I acrobat
between the two.

I've read more books
than I've had girlfriends.
Loneliness
is a stubborn fellow,
only wants
to point you
in the direction
of your coffin.

Sometimes
my self-esteem dresses in black,
travels third class in my thinking.
Sometimes
I sit on a park bench
and watch
the branches of trees
wafer
the morning light.

Each human being
caught between
time
and desire.

Cross the continent
of a room
to say "Hello again"
to someone
who'll be
indifferent.

Snail shell,
heartbreak.

OPEN CITY

So you
blindfold the days
with sleep.

Fog
is
fog,
not healing.

Laundry
becomes
a mountain.

Behind
the mountain,
a knock.

A friend
with ear and heart.

You talk
a river.

Dawn.
The clock
extracts
a sliver
of laughter.

The mirror
asks you
for
yet one more
beginning.

Portrait of an Artist's Studio

Lucy Cavendish

OPEN CITY

Open City my ass. "Open" means you are rich and white and did good drugs in the past twenty years. "City" means you live in Manhattan and you bought your loft with your Trustafundian money. I see, it's a code . . .
    (Letters, page 241)

Heart Machine Time

Bill Broun

Alcohol gave me wings to fly,
Then it took away the sky.
—from *Alcoholics Anonymous*

MARTIN, A MAN I SPONSOR IN AA, CALLS MY CELLULAR PHONE TO say he is cleaning his underwear in his kitchen sink. He acts like I'm to blame for this situation.

"You don't understand how bad off I am," he says, "You don't know."

"I think you sound pretty bad, Martin." I have to shout. I'm on an airport tarmac, close to the International Terminal. Heat ruffles up from the ground, making the brownish pink clouds near the horizon quiver and glisten. Jet engines scream around me. "Hold on," I say. I put the phone on the pavement. The jets sound like circular saw blades shot at me from all directions. I yank a bag stitched with swirled flowers from a moving belt—the end of a load from Paris. I chuck it into the last cart on the cart train, and pick up the phone again. I get on the belt motor—a sort of drivable ramp, like a giant cardiac exerciser on wheels—and pull out.

I say, more humanly, "Stay with me just a minute more, Martin."

"This isn't that important," he says. "I'm being a baby."

"Just wait!"

I head back, trying to cradle the phone on my lap. I swerve under a wing, ducking, then coast into the enormous Quonset hut called the baggage bank. I drive toward the square opening in the cargo floor,

"Hades," where we shove the suitcases and hat boxes, the ski poles and sticky baby chairs. The bags all ride the underground conveyor until they pop onto the chrome merry-go-rounds where passengers grapple.

This morning we moved three hundred frozen cobras for a veterinary college. Each snake costs a fortune. They'd come from a laboratory in India, via Charles de Gaulle. Another ramp rat, Jimmy K., broke open one of the flight cartons for us. "Oops!" he mocked, ripping off the first of the tape. Then he went wild. "Oops, oops, oops!" No one laughed though. One by one, we all took our look. The snake came in clear bag of blue jelly, like a spiral in a marble. It was small and pale, almost a worm. It gave us all this bad feeling. Personally, I didn't think the prank was too funny; in sobriety, in AA, we're supposed to play by society's rules. But I didn't want to nark on Jimmy, plus, he'd start one of his rants—about our low pay, how they deserved it. I quietly went back to work. I felt all confused and guilty, slamming suitcases around like bricks in Hell, and finally I had to call my own AA sponsor, Buzz. Buzz said, "One snake? Let it go."

"But won't I be some kind of accomplice?"

"If this Jim character had taken five or six snakes," said Buzz, "I'd say report him. One cobra? Just forget this. It's a matter of proportion. And remember: You're mainly responsible for yourself. You can't fix the world."

I told Buzz, "Thanks, Buzz. Thanks for being Buzz." And I was grateful for my sponsor.

After break, Jimmy, looking worried, carefully bundled the rubbery snake and the membranous mess into Taco Bell food wrappers. He thrust it all deep into a white plastic F.O.D. bucket, which is, weirdly enough, for "foreign object debris." I still felt distracted—"too into myself," as Buzz would say. So I was actually glad when, during our next plane, Martin called.

"I think my intestines are sort of rotting or something," he says now.

I say, "I believe you, Martin."

He has been defecating all over his apartment this morning. He's spilling a lot of blood, too, yet he refuses to go to the hospital. What can you say? This is what happens to Martin after just two days of drinking nowadays. But I'm only making an educated guess when I say, "Martin, I think if you don't stop drinking you're going to die."

You should see Martin. He's handsome, with icy blue eyes and the boxy chin of a fairy tale prince. He has three interesting nervous "habits," besides alcoholism. One is that he blinks frequently. The second is puckering his forehead and parting his lips slightly before he speaks. Together, they give him the appearance of someone trying to drink from a fire hydrant. The third habit—I'll get to that.

At age thirty-nine, Martin is a failed actor. He's also one of these people who seems to both punish and pathetically elevate himself by reminding you of his failures, the more agonizing the better. He lives off his parents, who send money from Massachusetts. His claim to fame at our AA meetings is he doesn't believe in God.

We once told him: "No one's asking you to worship any god." We told him—we were kind of holier-than-thou, I recall—all about the New York City atheists who helped start AA. In London, we said, there were still meetings where they'd bawl you out if you dared mention God. "See, you can be an atheist and it's OK."

He shook his head and started blinking. He has this way of making our platitudes seem like spiteful ploys. He said, "Now you guys are getting creepy. And that's all I'm saying." Yet Martin kept coming around to Commonwealth House, sitting on the back couches. He wanted to be left alone, he made clear. But he "kept coming back," as we AAs say. Once, after the third or fourth time he relapsed, I saw him berate himself for letting down his family. "Don't get your hopes up for me," he said. "I think I'm doomed. I'm a piece-of-crap son and I don't deserve help." Of course, in AA, these sorts of words are supposed to grab your conscience. So I made it my mission to be Martin's friend.

Now he's saying, "I've got it coming out both ends." I hear him pause, taking a deep breath. "First I noticed blood in my vomit, just some red bits. Then it started coming up like motor oil." He makes a sarcastic *phuuu* noise through his teeth, like static on Radio Nowhere. "It was fucking horrible."

I can't think of what to say. Martin never accepts my sympathy. What he wants are eyewitnesses. So I say, "Wow."

"I'll be OK," he says. "Don't get upset. I'm going to stay put."

I say, "Why can't you just let a doctor check you out?"

"No doctors," he says. "I know what they'll do. They'll shove me through all their neato machines!" He says it like that, like a punch line. "Ha! No. No way. Ha!" I've imagined the dark mental screening room in Martin's head, with its wry, blinking audience of other Martins in seat rows, each with their auburn hair parted perfectly on the side. There's a grim nervousness in there, too. You hear it throughout Martin, seismic tremors far beneath Movie Land, making all the sulky Martins restless in their seats.

"How do you feel right now?" I say. Through a wall, I hear the intercom in the terminal, an echoey monotone, like a snail's song. "I mean, right this second?"

"I don't know how I feel—trapped. I've got the shakes," he says. "I know the shakes. I'll be alright. I'm just not having loads of fun."

Last year, for a little while, Martin and I seemed to have a nice time together. He was terribly lonely, and, really, I was too. We'd sit at his computer, firing violet-red rays into space aliens shaped like ripply tusks. We knew it was stupid, but we couldn't stop. I'd hit the key marked "CTRL" and he'd commandeer the ship with his joystick, offering pessimistic commentary. "This is a Cyberian ambassador ship. It's not supposed to attack us, but . . ." Or, "This pulsar will drag our engines down. Just watch." Then, one night, we got tired of the game. He went to the kitchen to make us coffee. I heard him talking on the phone. He was checking on Sabro, another AA who couldn't often stay sober very long. Poor Sabro has no hands, but flippers. When we say the Lord's Prayer at the end of our meetings, I sometimes get to hold Sabro's flipper. It is a beautiful thing to grasp, like a limb too perfect for earth. You can almost feel the ghost hand in it, swimming nimbly in its flawless world.

Martin came back holding his heavy chin high, out like an elbow. It was as if he was finally in charge of something.

"Sabro's OK," Martin said curtly. "He just needs someone to talk to."

I could tell Martin really loved Sabro, and after talking about Sabro, we got on the subject of how it was, if anything else, good to have friends.

"And you're good, too," I told him. "I think you're a really good person trying to break out."

Martin's face got red. "Don't hand me too much of this formalized intimacy stuff, OK?"

"I'm sorry," I said. "What I'm trying to say is, I like you."

"Well, you don't have to force it."

That night, amazingly, I almost convinced him to go with me to this chapel I know about, a place for people like him and me. It's a giant cube painted maroon inside.

"We won't pray," I promised. "We'll just sit and soak up whatever's there."

Martin had said, "Hmm." He'd made with his blue lips the softest smile.

But instead of going, Martin brought out a messy stack of photographs of himself in films I'd never heard of. Some of them fell on the carpet and he left them there. He handed them over and sat on his couch. "Get ready. You're in for a laugh," he said. I took a slow look. There was a flash of a thinner, younger version of Martin in loose swim trunks, feeding a dark fish to a happy dolphin in a pool. There was Martin as a dismal chauffeur, opening a limo door for a tall women in foxes. The one I remember most was Martin as a medieval monk, he and his jug of holy water getting whacked aside by two bearded men who battled with broadswords. The water flew into the air like a visible shriek. There was something that went beyond the cliché of that image, Martin's princely face and long, gentle mouth, its surprise and weariness and insult. In all of them, Martin was decidedly placed at the edge of each frame. I laughed alright, but they were sharp, hard little laughs.

Now he says, bitterly, "At this point, if this binge kills me, that's fine. That's perfectly fine." Then he adds, "You won't have to worry about old Martin anymore. That ought to make your life a lot easier, huh?"

I say, "Don't."

And that's it. He hangs up forever, for Martin's third habit is trying and not trying to stage suicide attempts. What I heard later was that Martin drunkenly swallowed a bottle of aspirin. He was already hemorrhaging, and the aspirin did him in. He'd tried to walk out into the street and stop a car. They found him beside the building, in a parking lot of asphalt cracked to pieces.

That day—it wasn't so long ago—turned out to be a very hard one. It was more than Martin.

A fairly young DC-10, one I'd helped cargo, was taking off for Mexico City International on Runway Eighteen. We were on break in the baggage bank, eating our lunches, playing dominoes. Because we'd removed our headphones, we heard the bang. We'd have heard it anyway. It sounded like a car backfiring, only ten times louder. We jumped. Everybody jumped. Jimmy K. dropped a box of dominoes. The black rectangles bounced off the shiny floor. By the time we sprinted out of the hut, the fire engines were screaming bloody murder and racing toward the end of Eighteen.

I hopped on my motor and speeded toward the plane. This wasn't exactly authorized, but something took over in me. Already, the bright yellow inflatable chutes were dangled out the sides of the DC-10, their segments trembling in the wind. Men and women in silver suits unraveled long white hoses from the fire trucks. Passengers burst down the slides. Nothing was calm or orderly about it. You can imagine. I could see the plane was OK. No smoke, no fires. Perhaps a gull had flown into an engine. Just a scare. But the passengers, mostly men in dark suits, they didn't care. They were way beyond any suggestions. They hit the ground, then scrambled from the plane.

I got to about two hundred yards from the plane and stopped. I stayed on the grass median, a bumpy area riddled with rabbit holes. There are regulations for cargo personnel. For some reason, one desperate woman spotted my belt motor and its tilting ramp and, of all the vehicles shooting toward the plane, thought I was the kind of help she needed. She looked about forty. She wore a light green dress, but was barefoot. Her dark hair was still styled into neat, lustrous waves. She ran toward me and my ramp, waving her arms. Her face was twisted horribly. She screamed, "Please, O God!" She fixed her huge eyes on my face.

I suddenly got this mental picture of Martin, lying on his shit-covered couch beside a carton of elderberry wine. Of course, I didn't know Martin was really going to die at this point. I don't know. I wanted to pull the ramp back, away from the woman, to step on the accelerator and get out of there and not look back.

But the woman clambered onto the seat and clutched the safety bar. It was as if she'd just caught the last subway from the edge of the earth. She turned one of her brown forearms over and over, flexed her fingers in and out. She bent down and checked her feet. She looked at all the body she could see, panting. She kept fidgeting. But she never took both hands off the chrome bar at the same time.

I didn't know what to say. So I said, "I just unload the bags." She didn't say anything to that. She looked at me like I was nuts. Then, somehow, she bumped the lever with the green ball on its end and the belt on the ramp started trundling upwards.

We rode toward the terminal, not talking, the belt rolling, and you know—I wondered about her bags. This is what I remember. I knew we wouldn't get to touch the DC-10 for hours. It was silent and breezy. I felt very lucky to be alive and yet sad about Martin hanging up on me. There was going to be a long break this afternoon. All the other planes had stopped flying.

When I parked the ramp, the woman just sat there, staring around the baggage bank. "How can I help you?" I asked. She said nothing. She shook her head no. She glanced up, into the cave-like ceiling with its shadowy green trusses showing like faint ribs. When a jumbo takes off, the roof screeches a bit and shudders, and it feels like being inside Godzilla. But all you could hear now was the squeaking sound of the rollers on my belt motor. The woman had both hands on the safety bar. It became clear she wasn't going anywhere. And then I had a funny impulse. I climbed up onto the rumbling belt, stood up and started walking down it—walking in place. It's a regular joke with the ramp rats. It's our secret. We call it Heart Machine Time. It's only six feet high, so no one gets hurt. But I'd never tried it before. Of course, Heart Machine Time was one of Jimmy K.'s specialties; and now here I was, Mr. Law and Order, making long uncertain strides. "Hey, look at this," I told the woman. "It's heart machine time." I tried to make a sweet face. I tried to walk the weirdness out of the situation. "You walk and you get better." I said something Jimmy K. always says: "The doc says my heart is breaking. So it's heart machine time." She took one unsure hand off the bar and wiped her nose. A glistening streak ran along her cheek. The other rats stood around, watching, pulling on their green reflector vests. Some of them smiled and some didn't. There'd almost been a major airline disaster, after all. Yet Jimmy croaked, "You got it!" He turned a lever, and the belt really started hustling. "Is this boy going to live?" he said. The woman glanced quickly at everybody's faces, and then she cracked a tiny, shocked smile. "You muthafuckers is crazy," she said. I began to trot down the moving belt, faster and faster. I could barely breathe. I imagined Martin blinking at all this, scrunching his forehead, opening his mouth to condemn the God none of us understood. Maybe I felt I'd never been enough for my poor friend, and somehow I knew he was going away from us that day. But I wanted to get distance from him. I wanted to be happy. That's what I remember most. I couldn't bring myself to jump off because I felt like something was almost chasing me toward joy. I wanted to run, down and down the ramp. Then, stop, and ride the belt back up toward the edge.

Devil's Grass

Margaret Ricketts

This time has
been, will be
the season
of a nasty
reckoning,
of sobs smothered
in public bathrooms
on
toilet paper,
the season of broken
stems,
of tumors and burdens.
You ask what now,
what next, and I
want to conjure
up a compassion as slow,
intense and urgent as the
devil's grass slowly ripping
up the seams of the pavement

After dinner, he checks the hydrometer in the bathtub. The water is just right so he takes a bucket to the living room. He sucks on the siphon to get it going and accidentally takes in a salty mouthful. He spits it into the empty bucket. Then he gently pours in some new water as old water runs through the siphon, filling the empty bucket.

Octo watches him calmly. He's used to all this.

(McIntyre, page 27)

A Set for an Opera About Plants

Ena Swansea

OPEN CITY

Sitting around a low table are five people Rose can only describe as being in their early twenties.
(Reagan, page 61)

The First of Your Last Chances

John McNally

MY GIRLFRIEND PATRICE POINTS AT A CLOUD AND SAYS IT LOOKS like a cow. Another day, it's the profile of a lumberjack. Occasionally, the image gets more complicated: a fat man walking his poodle, or the head of a famous statesman, Winston Churchill or Henry Kissinger, hovering ten thousand feet above us.

"Look," she'll say. "Mousy Tongue."

"What?" And then I'll remember: It's a nickname, a pun in her vast repertoire of puns. "Ah, yes," I'll say. "Got it! Mao Tse-tung. Of course, of course."

"See him?"

"Nope."

Two days ago, she saw my mother holding a spatula.

"Do you see her?" she had asked. "Right there—see that dark streak? That's her bottom lip. You know that look she gets? That's it to a tee, Michael. It's amazing."

But I couldn't see it. Patrice's clouds are not my clouds. It's been four weeks since we've had sex, and what I see each time I look up is raw carnality: clouds humping clouds, or long cumulus erections floating overhead, ominous as zeppelins, swallowing us with their shade.

"I'm sorry," I said, "but I don't see my mother up there."

"Really?"

"Really."

At work, Darren tells me he's recorded a voice-mail ad for himself in the personals. He's just a kid, turned nineteen last month—a tall, skinny, hollow-eyed college dropout. His cigarette is jammed in the corner of his mouth, and each time he speaks, he fills the cab of the truck with thick blue-gray smoke.

"They've got these different categories," he says. "*Looking for Love, Unusual Appetites, Three's Company.*"

I crank down the window, suck in a lungful of fresh air.

"So I recorded one under *All Tied Up,*" Darren says. "For laughs, you understand."

"*All Tied Up,*" I say. "And what was your message?"

"Oh, Christ, I don't know. 'Looking for a woman who can tame this beast.' Something like that." He's smiling and laughing, but there is genuine fear in his eyes. The reason he's telling me this is because he wants reassurance that what he's done is okay, but I won't give him any. When he realizes this, he says, "I've got my first date. Saturday afternoon." He says this quietly, almost as an afterthought.

"Hey, hey!" I say. "Congratulations."

Darren is hunched at the wheel, so I clap him on the back. My burst of enthusiasm perks him right up. "Her name's Tova," he says. "Get this—she asked if I was a dom or a sub."

"And?"

"I said, sometimes a dom, sometimes a sub. Depends on my mood."

"Good answer."

He squints through smoke and says, "You think?"

"Absolutely," I say. "When in doubt, straddle the fence."

Darren snuffs out his cigarette, and in a rare moment of self-confidence, he grins at me and says, "That ain't all I'll be straddling, pal."

After it gets dark, I carry a coat rack up from my truck to my apartment. I'm head of University Surplus—our job is to lug away whatever the departments don't want and offer it once a week to the public at a reasonable price—and every night for the past five years I've taken a little something home for myself, a bonus for making it through another day. Yesterday it was a file folder from the Department of Mortuary Science and Funeral Service. Today it's a coat rack from a dean's office. Tomorrow we're removing every last item from the old Student Health building, which is scheduled for demolition, and I've got my eye on a magazine rack from the waiting room. What I'd *really* like is a water fountain—we have three of them—but I haven't yet figured out the logistics for hooking one up inside my apartment.

After dinner, I go to Patrice's. She lives across the street from Wrigley Field on the top floor of a brownstone. Clearly, I have done something wrong—I have erred in any of a thousand ways—but Patrice won't tell me what I've done. Whatever it was, though, it happened a month ago, and this is why the sex has been cut off. Any minute now I expect Patrice to give me an ultimatum. She has a pun for this, too. *Ultimatum* becomes *old tomatoes*, as in, "They've been living together for five years, so Marcy finally gave Jack the old tomatoes: marry her or move out." Like Mousy Tongue, the old tomatoes is part of another language, a language with a past I can't quite wrap my brain around. It's another Patrice from another time in her life talking to people I've never met. Nonetheless, I see the old tomatoes coming, and I'm prepared to duck.

Outside Patrice's window is a gorgeous view of Wrigley Field. I'm in the middle of moping, staring mindlessly at the empty ballpark below, when Patrice walks over and starts mussing my hair, what's left of it. She pushes it around until the top of the fringe that surrounds my head curls up onto the bald spot like a pair of horns trying to sprout. I read this as a sign of forgiveness, but when I try to return the touch, a brush of thumb against her breast, she grabs my wrists and leans back, surveying her work. Patrice is a Classics major at Northwestern, and what she's doing is fashioning me into a famous Roman.

"So," I say. "Who am I?"

"What do you mean?"

"I mean, which Roman am I?"

Patrice opens her mouth, but the first vibrations of an approaching train stop her from speaking. It's the Evanston Express roaring up from the Belmont stop south of us. Patrice's apartment is so close to the tracks, I could lean out her window, if I felt like it, and knock on the passing train's windows. Every time a train goes by, it's an event around here. First, pots and pans rattle. Then the leaded glass of Patrice's bay window starts to shiver in its sockets, thrumming harder and harder. Then the beast itself appears—whistle blowing, metal grinding against metal, showers of sparks thrown at us from the hot rails. Eventually, the last car blasts past us, and the train snakes around another apartment building, disappearing from view. This happens several times an hour, all day long and most of the night.

"Wow," I say when it's over. "It's like friggin' Cape Canaveral around here. How do you stand it?"

"Stand it?" she asks. "How do I stand *what*?"

"Living here," I say.

Patrice lets go of my wrists and glares at me. I'm in trouble again, so I try steering us back on course. "Hey!" I say. "You never told me who I am. I'm a Roman, right? Come on, Patrice. Tell me. Who am I?"

"Nobody," she says. "You're nobody." Then she heads for the kitchen.

"We talked dirty on the phone last night," Darren says. Darren speaks out of the corner of his mouth, the corner without his cigarette, but the cigarette still bobs up and down with each syllable.

"Watch where you're walking," I say. "Keep your mind on work." We're carrying a gynecological examination table out of Student Health. It's the fifth one we've moved this morning, and I am now acutely aware of all the never-before-used muscles in my body, muscles which feel prodded with sharp instruments one second, then set ablaze the next. There are fifty-two rooms in Student Health—four of which are large waiting rooms—and we need every last thing cleared out of here by Monday morning before the wrecking ball strikes the east wing.

Darren says, "I've never talked dirty before. I mean *really* dirty."

"Why do you think I'm interested," I say. "Why?"

"She asked me if I've ever done a woman in the, you know, in the *butt*."

I get a better grip on the table by looping each of my arms underneath a stirrup. I grunt, heave the table higher.

Darren wiggles his end of the table through a door frame. "Do you and Patrice ever talk dirty?"

"Patrice does. But that's just how she is. She talks dirty to everyone."

Darren and I stop when we reach Betty. Betty is the better of our two dump trucks—reliable, most days; Veronica, on the other hand, is sluggish, unpredictable, sometimes hard to start. My other two workers are loading Veronica full of cabinets with sliding glass doors, each cabinet as heavy as a pool table.

"I bet Betty here talks dirty," I say, lowering her lift. "Don't you, honey?" We scoot the exam table onto the lift, then I hit the lever so we can ride up with it. The back half of the truck is already cram-packed full of shit—waiting room furniture, upright scales, even the rubber torso of a woman, apparently for teaching breast self-examination techniques.

Darren flips the butt of his cigarette out the back of the truck, and without warning, he breaks into his impression of Tova: *"I want you to take that nice big throbbing cock of yours,"* he says, *"and I want you to stick it as far up my hairy ass as you can get it."*

Two undergraduate girls appear just then from between Betty and Veronica. They are on their way to class, taking a short cut across campus, thick books clutched to their chests. They glance quickly into the dark cavern of the truck, and when they see the two men inside—one hollow-eyed and talking dirty, the other sweaty and out of breath—they turn away quickly and pick up their pace.

Darren chuckles sheepishly. He fiddles with the stirrups, then stops what he's doing and says, "Just what the hell are these things for anyway? I've never seen them on any examination table *I've* been on." He wiggles the stirrups again, pushing them in and out of the table, the way a bored child would.

I reach over, take hold of Darren's chin, and playfully wag it back and forth. "You're in over your head, my friend," I say. "Way over."

After work, I sit in the darkened office and read through the print-outs of our stock. We always have more discarded items than we have room to store—too many dormitory desks, too many chairs, too many outmoded computers and achingly slow dot-matrix printers. This is the hour when I decide what I'm going to take home. Will it be an oscillator today or will it be a set of free weights? Pyrex beakers or a swing-arm lamp? *This* or *that*? I'm never at a loss for things to choose from. The fact is, enough junk passes through here in a year's time to furnish a small country.

I settle on one of the small jewels of Surplus: a Bell and Howell sixteen-millimeter projector. The mere sound of its chugging sprockets and clicking shutters is enough to lull me back to grade school, all those long mornings spent slouching in webs of light while grainy films about photosynthesis, Stranger Danger, and reproduction danced and jerked before our eyes.

I carry the projector out to my truck, then return to Surplus. After some digging, I find a box of empty reels, two new projector lamps, and a stack of Biology films about a fictional guy named Joe.

When I arrive at Patrice's apartment, she buzzes me in, but by the time I climb the stairs up to the third floor, she's already in the shower. I turn the Cubs game on and wait. The game on TV is the exact same game being played right outside Patrice's window at Wrigley Field. I hate baseball, actually, but I decide to do an experiment. I try to see if I can detect the millisecond delay in the broadcast. When the crowd outside the window roars over a nicely executed play, the crowd on TV roars as well. So here I sit: ear toward the TV, thumb on the remote control's volume, hoping to catch a moment so small it boggles the mind.

This is the sad way I occupy my time these days instead of having sex. Patrice is in the shower, and just a month ago I'd have been in there with her . . . *Patrice's back mashed up against the tub surround, her right leg raised and jutting out, the ball of her foot pressing down onto the tub's edge to give her some leverage while I move in and out of her, in and out.* This is how things used to be around here: *panties, still warm in the crotch, resting on the floor,* a sight that rarely fails to get me hard. But not anymore. Nope. I am reduced to watching a sport I hate and acting like a child. Another month, and I'll be outside plucking apart grasshoppers and poking sticks mindlessly into sinkholes of mud.

"Hey," I yell. "Is everything okay in there? You turned into a prune yet or what?"

No reply. Half an hour has come and gone, and Patrice is still in the shower. Then José Hernandez hits a home run for the Cubs, and the crowd roars loader than ever. There is no difference, I decide, between real time and TV time, so I give up my project. I turn to the picture window, hoping to see the ball as it soars out of the park and onto Waveland Avenue, but as soon as I lean closer, the window's glass explodes into the apartment, causing me to duck and fall out of my chair. For a second I think it's José Hernandez's ball that has smashed the window, but when I regain my balance, I see that it's a rock the size of a golfball. I poke my head out the broken window and catch a glimpse of the culprit, a grown man. He's running down the street, looking every so often over his shoulder, making sure no one's on his heels. I'm about to yell, but he turns a corner and disappears from my sight.

Patrice steps from the bathroom wearing a robe I've never seen, an extra-fluffy salmon-colored towel wrapped swami-style around her head. She doesn't seem to notice the shattered glass all over her living room. All she notices is *me*. She stares a bit, then yawns and says, "Oh. You're still here. Well, I need to paint my toenails," she says. "So if you'll excuse me." And then she is gone again, locked in the bathroom, leaving me once more to my own devices.

I sweep up the glass, seal the rock up inside of a Ziploc baggie, and set it on the kitchen table with a note (EXHIBIT A, it reads). Then I take the A/B train home.

Saturday morning, Patrice and I take a stroll through Lincoln Park while two men we don't know fix her window.

"They'll steal your CDs," I say.

Patrice shrugs.

"They'll take your TV," I say.

She shrugs again.

"Okay," I say. "It's your junk, not mine. Want to go to the zoo? The monkeys are always worth the price of admission."

"Monkey shmonkey," Patrice says.

"Not in the mood to visit the relatives today? So be it," I say.

We plop down onto a park bench, deciding our next move. Patrice leans her head back, and I figure she's soaking in the sun when she says, "That big cloud? Right there?" She points.

"What is it?" I ask.

"Hairy ass," she says.

"Really!" I say. At long last, I think. Abstinence has finally taken its toll on Patrice. We are riding the same wave. We are both seeing sex where there is no sex.

Patrice squints, shades her eyes, and says, "Hairy Ass Truman."

"Ah," I say. "Of course." First, Mousy Tongue; now, Hairy Ass.

"The cloud next to it?"

"Yes?" I say, but I am tired of her antics, tired of funny names and pointless cloud gazing.

Patrice turns to me and says, "It looks like *you*." She says this like an accusation.

I look up, and for once I see what she sees. The cloud *does* look like me. But it also looks like I'm wearing a fedora, and it would appear that I have a hard-on that's roughly twice as long as I am tall.

"And look," Patrice says. "Gerald Ford's over there. Sort of hovering behind you."

But now I'm lost again, unable to see anything other than myself.

"Gerald Ford," I say. "Now, *there's* a fascinating man, if you ask me. Here's a guy who forgave Nixon for his crimes. Nixon! Of all people! Ford found it in his heart to forgive this awful, evil man." I say all of this without any pretense of subtlety. The man who broke Patrice's window, I've decided, is her new lover, and what I need from Patrice is forgiveness, even if it means forgiveness for crimes I can't remember committing.

"It's called a pardon," Patrice says. "Ford pardoned Nixon, and I'm sure it was agreed upon before Nixon resigned. Part of the deal, I imagine."

I stand from the bench. I pace back and forth, then stop in front of Patrice. "I know what this is about. The old tomatoes, right? Don't tell me it's not. You're going to give me the old tomatoes. Am I right?"

I am saying all of this louder than I mean to, and people are watching us. They are watching *me*.

"Okay," I say. "Okay, okay. What did I do? I can't take this anymore. Tell me, would you? Tell me what I did so you can pardon me and we can move on."

"Why should I tell you if you can't remember?"

"Why?" I say. *"Why?"* Her question is a preposterous follow-up to my question, but I store it away as evidence—*concrete evidence*—of the difference not just between Patrice and myself, but between all men and women, from Adam and Eve to every last couple, fat and thin, young and old, here with us today in Lincoln Park.

I soften my voice and ask one last time: "Why?"

Patrice narrows her eyes. She says, "Does the word *fudge* mean anything to you?"

"Fudge? Are you saying I *lied* to you about something? Is that it? I fudged the truth?"

Patrice lets out a deep, hoarse sigh. It is a sigh of disgust, a sigh of finality. She stands and gathers her belongings. "Look," she says without looking at me. "I need to get going. My paper on the Triumvirate is due on Monday."

Patrice walks away, and I yell to her back, "I have *never* lied to you. Do you hear me? Never!"

Only after Patrice is gone and I have made a public spectacle of myself do I understand the fudge she means. My apartment is across the street from a shop called The Fudge Pot—they specialize in expensive fudge and chocolate—and a month ago Patrice gave me a twenty-dollar bill to buy her a brick of Turtle Deluxe. Two days later I found that same twenty dollar bill crumpled in the front pocket of my jeans, and I had thought, *A windfall . . . Too good to be true!* Here was twenty dollars I couldn't remember—a miracle, it had seemed, since I had less than ten bucks left to my name and payday was still a week away.

"Jesus Christ," I say. *"Fudge!"*

But it's not the fudge that's gotten to her. I realize that now. Fudge was merely a clue, a fingerprint attached to the larger issue at stake, and the only reason Patrice even brought it up was so that I might figure everything out for myself.

On the day that Patrice had given me the money to buy fudge, she had also broached the subject of me moving in with her. "It just makes sense," she'd said, and she started to tell me how much money I'd save in rent, but I cut her off: "Tell you what. Let's talk about this when I bring your fudge over. We'll sit right here and gorge ourselves on the most expensive chocolate in the city and hash out this moving-in-together thing once and for all. Whaddaya say?" "Deal," she'd said, and I'd said, "Deal." And then I never brought the fudge.

I had forgotten about the fudge, truly, or else I wouldn't have been so surprised at finding the twenty bucks two days later. It's possible that I subconsciously pushed the fudge aside, and this may be so. This was *not* the first time Patrice had suggested that I move in with her; it *was*, however, the first time I had agreed to talk about. We had struck a deal! We may even have shook on it. But once the fudge was out of my mind, so was the deal. Until today.

"Ah, shit," I say. "Shit."

Parents move their children along. Couples look anywhere but at me.

"Shit, shit, shit," I say and throw my hands up and sigh.

There is a message on my answering machine from Darren when I get home. His afternoon date with Tova is over, and he's calling me from the emergency room at Rush-Presbyterian.

His voice, trembling, whispers from my machine: "I need a ride. And bring a soft pillow, would you?"

I am there in less than twenty minutes, watching the poor bastard limp toward my truck.

"Darren," I say, offering my hand, pulling him up into the cab.

"Ow, ow, *easy*."

"What happened?" I ask.

"I need a drink," he says. "I need a drink to help the Darvocet go down."

"You really shouldn't mix—," I start to say, but Darren raises his hand.

We go to a bar called Smoky Joe's, and Darren sits quietly, wincing when he shifts from one haunch to the other. He shivers periodically and shakes his head as if trying to empty it—trying, I suspect, to shake off what must surely have been the horror show of his life, his date with Tova.

After an hour of silence and three shots of rail whiskey, Darren says, "It started out in good fun. I mean, hell, when she started talking dirty to me face to face, I couldn't *wait* for her to tie me to the bed. You'd have felt the same way."

"Of course," I say.

"I had one of those gags in my mouth. You know, the kind with the red ball. So I can't talk, right? And she says, 'I'm going to give you three chances to bail. I'll ask you three different times what you want me to do, and if you want me to stop, just wiggle the little toe on your right foot.' Simple enough, right? So she gives me my first chance right then and there, but since she hasn't done anything to me yet, I don't wiggle jack-shit. Then she does all sorts of, you know, *good* things to me, mostly with her tongue, so when she asks me the second time, I don't do anything again. Why would I? Hell, I was having a real bang-up time. Then she brings out the heavy artillery, and I start screaming my head off. Hot wax, whips, dildos—you name it. She even burnt me with my own cigarette." Darren opens his palm to show me, but I can't see much more than a blemish. He says, "She never asked me a third time. She never gave me my last chance."

"You're lucky she didn't kill you," I say.

"You're telling *me*," he says. "Swear to God, I thought it was check-out time."

We order more beer, more shots. Darren starts to light a cigarette, but once the lighter is in his hand, he thinks better of it, meticulously returning the cig to its pack and dropping the lighter back into his droopy shirt pocket.

"Jesus," I say. "This whole Tova experience, something like this'll probably sour you for good on dating."

"You'd think so, wouldn't you?" Darren says. "But I'm not so sure about that. I know you're not going to believe this, but it's opened my eyes. I was sitting in the emergency room and I started thinking, there's so much out there, so much shit I've never even *heard* about. It's weird, I know, but this whole experience brought that home for me. It made me realize that I haven't even scratched the surface yet. I don't know how to say this—I mean, Tova wasn't the right woman for me, but she unlocked this massive door of possibilities. *Infinite* possibilities, man."

"You're drunk," I say.

"No, no, I mean it," Darren says.

"I shouldn't have let you mix the booze and pills," I say. "Listen to yourself. A woman just rammed you with a dildo, and you're waxing philosophic on me."

"Okay," Darren says. "Whatever. But I don't see what's so goddamn exciting in *your* life that you think you can criticize *mine*." He lifts his drink and starts to lean back quickly in his chair, his cue to me that the conversation is over, but a sharp pain rockets through his ass, and Darren lets out a yelp that causes half the patrons to turn and look at us.

I'm pissed, but I don't say so. I stew instead. I can settle into silence like no one else I know. Part of why I'm pissed, though, is because Darren has unwittingly stumbled upon a few sad truths. What is so goddamn exciting in my life? Why do I think I'm in a position to criticize him?

"Excuse me," I say. On my way to the men's room, I stop at the pay phone and call Patrice. I get her answering machine, so I leave a message, telling her to meet me at my apartment at midnight, that we need to talk tonight, we need to hammer out, one way or the other, what's left of our future together. "The old tomatoes," I say and hang up.

Back at the table, I ask Darren if he can give me a hand. "I need to move a few things from Surplus to my apartment."

Darren lets out a loud stage laugh. "Are you kidding?" he asks. With much more caution this time, he leans back in his chair. Then he proceeds to wag his head at me and snort and look around the bar at the other patrons, all for dramatic effect. "Haven't you heard anything I've been saying?" he says. "I mean, look at me. I'm in pain. I can barely *walk*."

I remove four fifty-dollar bills from my wallet and slap them down in front of him.

"Okay," Darren says. "All right. What the hell."

Darren and I haul the last heavy item up to my apartment by nine o'clock. After Darren leaves, I shower and shave, and by the time Patrice knocks at the door just shy of midnight, everything is in perfect order, so I yell for her to come in.

"What's all this?" she asks. "What's going on here?"

I'm standing behind the Check-In partition, hands clasped on the counter. I'm wearing a long, white examination coat and a stethoscope around my neck. From the *Highlight's for Children* scattered about the room to the Norman Rockwell artwork on the wall, my apartment has been converted into a doctor's office, courtesy of Surplus and the old Student Health building.

Patrice reaches across the Check-In counter, lifts the stethoscope, and holds it to her mouth. "*You*," she says, "are a man with a loose screw. You realize that, don't you?"

"Do you have an appointment?" I ask.

She drops the stethoscope. She huffs and shakes her head. "Yeah; sure; why not?"

"Well then," I say. "Please have a seat." When she doesn't move, I point to the waiting room.

"This is too much," she says, but she does as she's told. She sits in the middle of a row of connected chairs. When she realizes that I'm not going to say anything right away, she crosses her legs and picks up a magazine, flipping through it once, quickly, then tossing it aside. She taps her fingers impatiently on the chrome of the chair's armrests. I open and close filing cabinet drawers, making a show of it, before flipping off the lights. "Hey!" Patrice yells, but I shush her. The old Bell and Howell sixteen-millimeter projector starts to chug, and a funnel of light shoots across the room. The shadow of Patrice's head floats on the screen behind her.

"Scoot down," I say.

Patrice looks over her shoulder, sees the eerie silhouette of her own head, then slides down onto the floor. The movie is a classic: *Joe's Heart*. It is one in a series of movies about Joe's various organs. I sit next to Patrice. I press my mouth against her ear and ask, "Are you here to see a physician?"

"I guess so," she says, playing along, seeming to get into the spirit of the night.

I loop a lock of Patrice's hair behind her ear, and while Joe's heart pounds around us, I lean in and kiss her cheek. "What do you think about Joe?" I ask softly. "He seems in pretty good shape."

Between kisses, Patrice says, "He should probably avoid strenuous activity. Too much stress on his hear—" we kiss "—might kill him."

"You think?" I ask.

"Absolutely," Patrice says.

"Here," I say. "I want you to follow me."

She hesitates. "I don't know," she says. "I don't think we should go to the bedroom."

"The bedroom!" I say. "Ha! What kind of a doctor do you think I am? That's the *examination room*. And I need to *examine* you. So please. Please do as I say. Let's not put up a fight."

Amazingly, she doesn't. She stands, and with one finger hooked into my collar, she tags along behind me.

"Wow," she says when I open the door. "Look at this."

The room has an examination table, pale-green cabinets, and three shiny canisters labeled for gauze, cotton, and tongue depressors. I say, "Please remove your clothes and slip into this." I hold out a thin pale-green gown with ties in the back.

The room's only window is open, the curtains are parted, and it is cooler here than in the rest of the house. Antiseptic. The lights are off, but there is moonlight to see by, moonlight and the play of light and shadow from the movie in the other room. Joe's heart thumps on, gently vibrating the floor. My own heart pounds away, beating, I realize, much harder and faster than Joe's.

"You'll feel better," I say, "once you've put this on."

Patrice takes the gown. She shrugs out of her sweater, then unlatches her bra. She uses the ball of one foot to remove the shoe of the other, then she wriggles free of her jeans. She is standing in front of me in nothing but panties and socks, and when she peels down the panties—silky fabric rubbing against thick ringlets of pubic hair—the friction creates static electricity, and blue sparks flicker and crackle between Patrice's legs. The hair on my arms lifts. In an instant, the air in the room has become dangerously alive.

"May I leave my socks on?" she asks. She is wearing white tube socks scrunched down to her ankles.

"You may not," I say. "The socks must come off as well."

She removes them using only her feet. "Okay. I'm sockless now," she says.

"Sockless indeed," I say. "Now up on the table." I pat the sanitary sheet that covers the exam table. "Upsy Daisy," I say. She tries being as gentle as possible, but the paper sheet still crunches beneath her. "Lean back," I say. "Relax. There you go. Now, put your feet in the stirrups." Patrice takes a deep breath. "Good, good," I say, once her feet are in place. "Now, scooch forward. That's right. Scooch right up to the edge of the table."

Joe's heart suddenly quits beating. The last of the film runs through the sprocket, and a blast of hot white light illuminates the living room, brightening our room as well. Patrice's gown is wadded up around her waist. Between her legs, she is wet and thick, as open and raw as a fresh wound, and I am about to touch her, to put a finger inside of her, but then I stop. "Mousy Tongue," I say. I reach over to a box of powdered rubber gloves and pull four out. I take the first one, wrap it around her left ankle and the stirrup, and tie it in a knot. A second glove keeps her right ankle from moving. I tie her wrists to the insulated pipes above and behind her head.

"You're going to torture me," she says.

"Nope," I say. "I'm going to *cure* you." I wheel over a table of surgical instruments, on which sets a pair of scissors. Starting from the bottom hem, working my way up to her neckline, I snip away the gown. Patrice is completely naked now and goose-pimpled in the chilly room.

"Do something to me," she says.

"I will," I say, and I lift the lid off the top of the tin canister labeled GAUZE. I reach in and pull out the first of what I owe her.

"What's that?" she asks.

"Turtle Deluxe," I say. "See these canisters? They're full of fudge. All three of them. Sixty dollars' worth of fudge, to be precise. Interest on your twenty bucks," I say. I hold the fudge near her mouth, but not close enough for her to reach it. Patrice lifts her head off the table, opens her mouth. "C'mon," I say. "Have some." Patrice tries touching the fudge with her tongue, but she fails. When I finally give her a bite, I stand back and watch her savor it. The noises she makes—deep groans of satisfaction—are the same noises she makes when I am inside her and moving slowly. She swallows the bite, licks her lips.

"We had a deal," she finally says.

"The fudge has arrived," I say. "The deal's back on."

"I want to make something perfectly clear," she says. "I'm going to give you one more chance, but there is a finite limit to how many chances I can give." She is shivering as she speaks. The veins beneath her skin are visible, and there is evidence in every soft tissue of her body that the blood inside those veins is pumping hard and fast. "Understood?" she asks.

"It seems to me," I say, "that you're the one tied up. I'm not sure that you're in the best position to negotiate."

"Well, look at you," she says. "If it isn't my little Caligula."

She shifts her focus to the fudge again and parts her lips. She strains to reach my hand, arching her back and stretching the rubber gloves. I let her take a huge bite this time, a bite nearly too large for her mouth.

"Is that enough?" I ask.

"No," she manages to say.

I give her yet another bite, though there is barely room for any more in her mouth. "Mmmmm," she says, and while she chews and swallows, dribbles of juice running down her chin, I slip out of my clothes. I ask her if she wants more, and she nods. I am standing between her legs. I lean forward and place the last of the fudge in my hand onto her tongue. Outside it is dark, the hoots and jeers of nighttime carousers drift up to the open window, and the clouds passing the moon look like clouds.

Mrs. Sherlock Holmes States Her Case

Jody Winer

Milk-chocolate sweeties sour his breath.
Tiny bubbles rise from his teeth
in their bedside tumbler.
His conversation's a soggy crumpet.
And don't get him started on the Pakistanis.
He adores Mum, Brighton in August,
sea awash with sewage, too cold to swim,
hotel brimming with red-faced widows.
Après bingo, their love moans fade the wallpaper.

A thick-skulled child, he spent days with birds,
binoculars slung from his ostrich neck,
shock of albino ankle above sagging socks,
fingers cradling a robin
sling-shot by someone smarter.

How can I get anything done?
Dog-faced Watson curled on the rug,
basset eyes fixed on my husband.
I think it's love. The fire dying,
both of them too lazy to stoke it.
Can't they pick themselves up,
solve something: Jack the Ripper,
hounds on the moors, whatever.
Back by dinner, boots caked with dung
and fox-death, heads in ether.
And those moth-food tweeds!

OPEN CITY

That damn hat! That pipe stench!
That magnifying glass he wouldn't need
were he not too vain for glasses.
And that stomach rash, what is it?

There's a war on. Science needs advancing.
But he's caught up in two-bit mysteries.
Let him unclog the kitchen drain,
put the children to bed
if he can remember their names,
our boys barefoot while he's shod
in Bond Street's bench-made best,
baffled I'm still here.

How to Arrive at a Motel

Jody Winer

Arrive in a swirl of fifties pearls,
toting mother's red leather hat box,
lips a violet, fists prim in white gloves.

Show up postmarked with poor grades,
low bowling scores, botched dentistry,
your story conceived in a 7-11 parking lot.

Or come alone in a rented car with nothing
but the price tag on your pink sweat suit,
hair fragrant with diner bacon.

Sign your real name. Smile like money.
Know the phone won't ring. Use the pool.
Don't ask how far to the next motel.

OPEN CITY

There is a large sign that says, "Just Say No!" on the door of William Burroughs's icebox with smiling Nancy Reagan underneath gazing thoughtfully at an automobile with the trunk open and two corpses stuffed inside it with their hands tied tightly behind their backs and neat bullet holes, one each through the right temple and one each through the crown of the head. "Professional job!" exclaim the mourners crowding around the open coffin, holding the neatly dressed children high for a better view.

(Taussig, page 69)

Who hath formed a god, or molten a graven image *that* is profitable for nothing?

—Isaiah 44, 10

Laura Resen

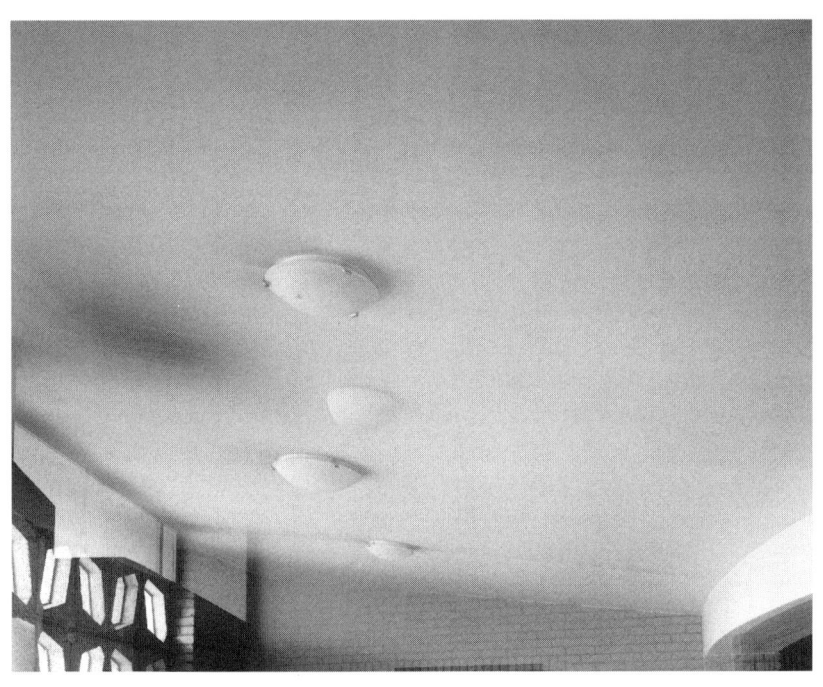

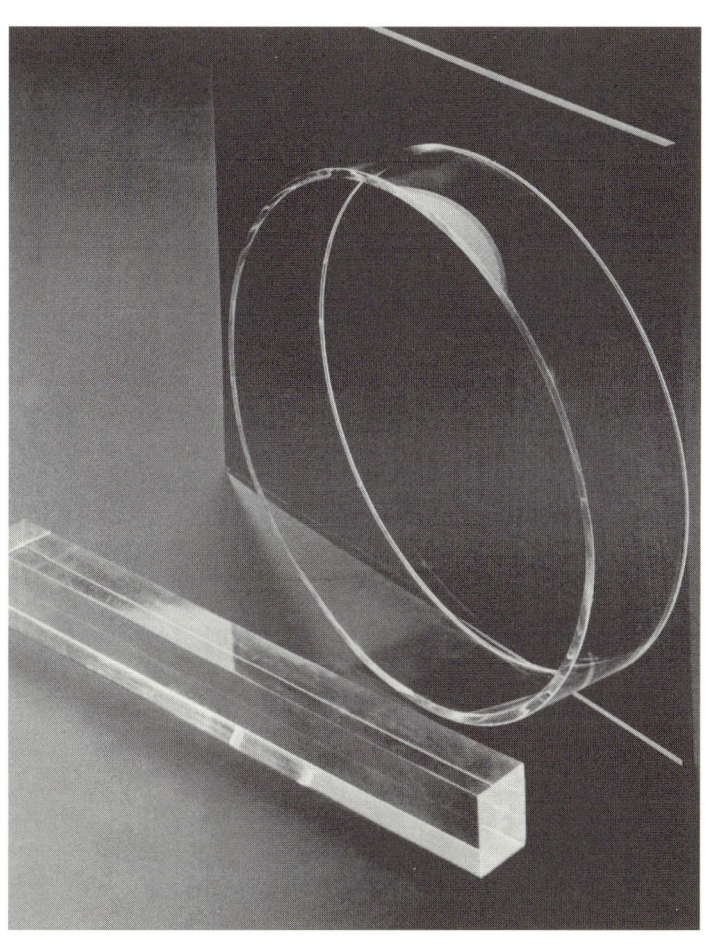

LaSalle

Andrea Reising

A very small
And surging thing
Nibbles at my heart
Dictating
What my body
Parts desire

I am silly sometimes
Sometimes I am blue
Sometimes I do things
I know I should not do
Sometimes I smoke cigarettes
And sometimes I drink beer
Sometimes when you're very far
I wish that you were here

OPEN CITY

Excuse me
Can I please
Acquit myself of Love
It is so daunting
To go through each day
Unsatisfied

Boyhood
Into womanhood
I go

Virgin Blue

Melissa Pritchard

1971

IRIS MET EVAN WHEN SHE WAS EIGHTEEN AND HE WAS TWENTY-five. They lived in a toolshed with an indigent's view of the sea, haunting the periphery of Santa Barbara's wealthy community in a yellow 1949 Cadillac named the Canary. They'd met during a guerrilla theater performance when Iris, lobbing balloons of fake blood against the steps of the downtown Bank of America, nailed, by accident or destiny, Evan's bare feet. He told her he owned a place near the university called The Dirty Bookstore. It was the size of a millionaire's walk-in closet, and while Evan knelt on a paisley cushion outside the store, concentrating on a Japanese board game calling for strategically imperceptible movements of smooth black and white stones, clients, older men, slouched past, trench coats belted, hats brimmed low. Iris once asked if there wasn't a costume shop around the corner that rented out the hats and trench coats. Paranoid about jail, Evan warned and rewarned his sole employee, a Vietnam vet named Lurch, not to sell to anyone under twenty-one, her for instance, he'd point out Iris, bundled in her Navy pea coat, black kohl snaked around her eyes, a shag haircut like Jane Fonda's in *Klute*. Evan enrolled in Russian language courses at the university and acted in most of their theater productions; in every play there seemed to be a part for a short conniver, a nasty jester. Now, Iris was nineteen and boiling over or broody, depending on the hour, with discontent. Evan had turned out to be much less than the local legend she had initially been enthralled by. He was fading local color, and Iris was putting up with him now, that's how she thought of it, putting up with, which sounded and felt wife-ish. His compulsive infidelities with costumers and prop girls along with his stock perversity, smacking Iris across her "cute, white ass" with a leather strap, were not, she reasoned, in her finest interest. Although living with Evan fixed the enemy as a perverse little man outside herself, still, her struggle for worth was perpetual, so chronic it verged on habit. Until now. Until this play she'd gotten a part in. Until Kellen. Until the part of Pam, a gabby British housewife who blew onstage in a rayon slip, chain smoking and grousing about her varicosed calves. But no matter. Iris was in love, the true kind which made her hope to exceed herself. She'd given up trying to locate an identity—a consistent self—and felt more like a vertical blank surface reflecting whatever was set before it, and now, with Kellen as her director, Iris, who only faintly aspired to be an actress, awaited an opportunity to shine him blindingly back to himself.

The play concerned a middle-class British couple whose daughter, Faith, renamed Joe Egg by the father in a moment's cruelty—*look at her, will you, she's just sitting around like Joe Egg*—had cerebral palsy. The couple's marriage suffers, the child suffers, hills and heaps of suffering all around—it was really a very grim play—with Kellen both director and mixed up father. No one in the cast, five altogether, minded much, since he was so personable. Kellen was the first nearly perfect person Iris had ever met—a contagion of joy poured off him, an ecumenical ledger of virtues and unassailable goodnesses. He was only twenty, a year older than Iris, and what she wanted was to so cunningly play herself he would fall in love with her, which meant falling more deeply in love with himself, the sort of trick Iris was best at. To that end, she thought of Park Haven, where she had worked once. (Despite its infusion of private monies and chilly, Italianate landscaping, Park Haven was little more than an institution, a storage bin. Inside, the staff padded about on chumpy white shoes; even the furniture looked clinically prescribed, like squares and buttons of aspirin.) After the cast's first read-through, when Kellen asked what any of them knew about cerebral palsy, Iris said nothing. She waited until everyone left before suggesting to him that the five of them visit Park Haven so the play would be more authentic, true to life.

In the middle of what Howard, Iris's stage husband, referred to as the "geek-gawk," Kellen befriended Joe Kerr, a young man writing his autobiography. Otherwise, the group visit had gone poorly. Once inside the vestibule of Park Haven, four of them—Iris, Marcia, Howard, and Audrey stood like a pasted-up lump of flesh, hinged together by the off-kilter British accents they were supposed to practice until the play opened. They were there to observe disability, chat up victims in wheelchairs, children afflicted with spastic paralysis (an old word, a staff nurse informed them, a garbage-can term sweeping into it anyone whose brain injury affected muscle control). Iris told no one she had worked one week in Park Haven's kitchen before being fired for shoving a blue waxed box of Snowcap lard in her purse—a joke for Evan. Just as she had been then, Iris was disquieted by Park Haven's bland Lutheran charmlessness, the linoleum's milky repellent sheen. In the lobby, floor-to-ceiling glass allowed a view of ponderosa pine, though even these, in their regimented rows, looked sinister, staged. So much fastidious polish suggested discouragement, erasures of quirk, the negating of distinctive wallows and spikes of personality. Color brochures, fanned out beside a bird-of-paradise arrangement on the receptionist's desk, called Park Haven home to sixty-five residents clearly routed there by way of exceedingly well-to-do relatives.

Shouldn't we be interviewing, Howard whispered to Iris, jotting down specifics of the disease, that sort of thing—some visible passport of purpose—he actually said that. Howard was an English major who "dabbled" in dramatics, wore polka-dot bow ties, and spoke like Iris didn't know what, a goofy professor. Holding, ticket-like, their Park Haven brochures, Iris, Howard, Marcia, and Audrey straggled over to the furniture in the lobby, seated themselves on Scandinavian chairs with nubbly, lime-green cushions. It was noon, with cafeteria noise floating down the hall, carrying with it a faint, pernicious smell of cabbage and boiled meat. With the guilt of the able-bodied, they watched Kellen lope up the hail from the cafeteria, six or seven children in wheelchairs surging around him. Audrey, the high school senior who played Joe Egg, mostly by slumping in her wheelchair and feigning an occasional rough seizure, gnawed her nails and muttered, Christ on a crutch. Howard, who on the drive back to the theater would repeat "poor buggers" numerous times as he stared glumly out the car window, finagled his face into a bright expression, utterly failing to disguise his distress at seeing such mangled bits, queerly knobbed birds of humanity. Only Marcia, who played Kellen's wife, seemed calm and unperturbed, kneeling like a relief worker to talk to several children at once. Iris worriedly looked about for the mean woman who had caught her stealing the lard, a Mrs. Peacock (who, it turned out, had been fired herself). And Kellen, displaying wholesome exuberance, slung his guitar off one broad shoulder, dropped cross-legged to the floor, and with children clustered in glinting metal nests all around him, began to sing. More children came wheeling down from various hallways while the staff, arms crossed, approving, hovered in the background—quite the nursery scrim, Howard's peevish comment.

They adored you. Marcia said, casting a worshipful glance of her own at Kellen as they all drove back to the theater. It was clear she hoped being his stage wife might work some alchemical influence, though everyone believed Kellen to be fatally besotted with Audrey's older sister, a cold dash of water named Yvette.

Right-O, said Howard in his wincingly stillborn Cockney. Obviously a Pied Piper. Still, their rehearsal that evening had unexpected energy. Audrey modeled her posture after a little girl she'd seen at Park Haven, and they all felt a more united sympathy for the characters, even for the ethically daft father, bent on murdering his daughter to shore up his marriage. The thing, said Kellen, was to keep improving their accents, which, he hated to remind them, were atrocious.

Two days later, Kellen took Iris with him to Park Haven to visit Joe Kerr. They were in Kellen's green VW bug, the dash heaped with wilted blue lupine and California poppy. Iris wore her newest thrift store finds, a parochial school blouse and vintage circle skirt, hand-painted labial pink with sudsy palm trees and a golden-eyed jaguar prowling the dirty hem. Kellen wore a blue workman's shirt, jeans, leather sandals, a blue headband knotted around his long, honey-brown hair. Iris had never known anyone so handsome, unaffected, kind. Solar exuberance, she put down in her journal, squiggling blue roses around his name, then scratching the whole thing out. Maybe certain people sieved right through language and were lost. Like the standard defense for a joke no one laughed at—you had to be there—you had to be in Kellen's presence to believe in unscathed happiness. It was as if he had never been harmed which is to say never born, and how could that be, didn't everyone protect themselves by practicing the subtler, meaner skills of growing up?

In the room he shared with a nine-year-old boy named Stigler, Joe Kerr had a metal desk and on top of the desk, a manual typewriter. Against the wall was stack of pink bakery boxes, holding, Joe said, his unfinished autobiography. While they waited for Dolores, his girlfriend, Joe demonstrated how he typed, clamping a pencil between his teeth, tapping each key. It took up to an hour to roll a piece of paper in and more than an hour, sometimes two, to write one page. He became enraged, he told them, when his thoughts shot past what his body could do. As Joseph Kerr II, he was the oldest son of a tool and die manufacturer in Chicago. His first five years were spent on the second floor of the family mansion in Winnetka until his parents were advised it would be best for everyone, particularly Joe, if he were sent here. Joe arched back his neck, laughing. I cramped their style. Here's the chapter I'm writing now. About Dolores. I call it "Fairy Tale." It starts with how she was dumped into a state hospital in Brooklyn, how her mother was told to take her to an institution, forget you had her, you've got other mouths to feed. Then—here's the fairy-tale part—last year, some cousin no one knew about died and left money so Dolores could go to a private home. Where she met me. Here she comes now. Hey. Dolores. Remember me telling you about these guys, the ones doing the play? You do? OK. He looked at Iris. Would you mind? Dolores needs the bathroom. It's down the hall to the right. Otherwise we have to call the staff nurse, and that can take forever.

Dolores was surprisingly heavy to push, and Iris, who had been told the week before at the public health clinic that she had a heart murmur, maneuvered the wheelchair into the ladies' room where she rolled down Dolores' large white cotton underpants, scooted her onto the toilet, waited, wiped her front and back, see-sawed her underwear back up around her waist, hefted her back into the wheelchair stuffed with rolled towels, clumps of clothing, cheap decorator pillows. Dolores was a big girl with lank, carob-brown hair, skinny, mink-colored eyes, thick glasses galaxied with dandruff, newsprint-colored skin, lips bunchy and chapped. Besides being big, Dolores was wrenchingly plain, so it was with a lurch of near-infatuation Iris saw Dolores's pubic hair, a black, glossy nest between the two forked branches of her legs. Iris was still seeing it, angling the wheelchair backwards, pushing out the door, breathless from her heart, still in love with that starry nest when she found Joe, in his Day-Glo wheelchair, waiting beside Kellen who came right over to help her.

Hey Iris. Joe says he's never been to the beach. Neither has Dolores. No one's ever taken them out of this place, so I just asked to borrow one of Park Haven's vans. Come with us tomorrow. I want you with us.

Evan had been nagging at her for weeks to make a skinflick, a blue movie for some people he'd met in L.A. Five hundred dollars for something you've done—hell, we've done—hundreds of times, Iris.

Not in front of the world. Not in front of strangers.

You're an actress. What's the difference?

Five hundred dollars—it would take months of waitressing and cleaning houses to save up that kind of money. She could take it and split for Mendocino. Mt. Shasta. According to Evan, his past girlfriend, who had flown over from London to study Japanese calligraphy and Gestalt therapy, had made enough movies to pay her way, first class, to India.

I have an appointment to meet with two producers down in Burbank tomorrow. Just to talk. You don't have to say anything. Or do anything. Just come with me.

As far as she could throw a stick, Iris didn't trust him. They'd get there and it would all be different from what he'd said. He'd convince her things were safe and when his promises got her going, he'd make her do whatever he wanted. Still. Five hundred dollars.

I can't. I'm going with some friends to the beach tomorrow. If you want, I'll think about it.

What's to think? What are you getting paid to do that play of yours?

Nothing. It's art.

Exactly. Well, guess what? You can make art and get paid. You've got a beautiful ass, Iris.

What's that supposed to mean?

It means I'm sick and twisted, the way you like me best. Evan dragged her down to the grimy mattress that didn't have sheets or pillows, just two old sleeping bags, the teeth so worn they didn't even zip together anymore. When he'd first brought her to the toolshed, Iris had been reading Dostoyevsky's *Crime and Punishment*. Evan, she thought, bore an uncanny resemblance to the murderer Raskolnikov, the ex-student in his filthy rags, brilliant, paranoid, repulsively handsome, full of mad plots. But Evan's filth had turned boring. And the literary depth had never existed, she had invented it.

Splitting a joint with Evan, Iris wound up talking about Joe, then how she'd helped Dolores in the bathroom, almost bragging she'd wiped somebody's ass for them. (Kellen was higher caliber, he wouldn't see that as anything special, just another joyful opportunity.) She was spacing out on Kellen, on the idea that a person of superior virtue could, unwittingly, make others feel inferior and thus find himself both resented and revered, when Evan started talking about one of his aunts back east who had had cerebral palsy, how his mother used to make him go with her on holidays to visit Aunt Margaret. Years later, he'd learned what a nightmare the state hospital had been for his aunt, how Margaret, with her bright mind, brighter than most, had been mixed in with imbeciles, hydroencephalics, people who ate their own feces, how three or four of them would be tossed like kittens into this big, high-sided box for what was called socialization, left in there all day, no matter what. Fascists.

What happened?

To my aunt? Starved herself. It took her years to die.

Iris could not believe how long it took to get Joe and Dolores out of Park Haven, into the pale-blue van and down to the beach. Half the day. The sand, where she'd poured a milk carton of seawater over it, shone like an uneven police badge of brown glass. Dolores's wheelchair was parked right off the end of a plywood board Kellen had slapped over the sand, end over end, like a thick, giant's playing card.

At first, Dolores, her face hidden under a puckered white canvas hat patriotically sprigged with tiny red flags, had been terrified by the crashing of the waves; her hypersensitive startle reflexes caused her arms and legs to shoot wildly about. Now she was quiet, her head lolling to one side, the wheelchair angled so she could see the water. Joe sat nearby in a sort of crooked W, his knees splayed beneath him. He wore Stigler's black swim trunks which were too small, and his white, extremely skinny chest and back were stippled with a bumpy red rash. Kellen, sitting nearby, had undressed Joe in the van, carried and set him down before helping Iris bring Dolores down. Iris unlaced Dolores's grimy tennis shoes, tugging them off, massaging each foot, working the flat arch, the soft heel, Dolores's sallow feet set loose from their canvas houses with the spoiled gray tongues. Squinting at Kellen through her gold, swan-shaped sunglasses, she imagined that like Dolores, she had never heard the sea's low, mournful chop or seen its wearying surface.

Joe was exuberant, windblown, hoarse from shouting over the moving green hills of the sea. He shouted to Kellen to carry him down to the water. Dolores, her head to one side, smiled without discernment, seeming to endlessly approve of anything Joe did. For this alone, Iris thought, Joe would be wild for her. Dolores was, he insisted, clever, slyly funny, though Iris had seen only the constant, almost creepy smile. Her cerebral palsy, he'd explained on the short drive to the beach, was much worse than his. She had hypotonicity or floppiness of the muscles, which meant she had trouble speaking, feeding herself, even using her hands. In her wheelchair, propped into a sitting position with rolled towels and pillows stuffed around her, a leather strap around her waist, she resembled a plump, broken-necked sparrow. Joe had an opposite affliction, hypertonicity, contraction of the muscles, so that he became rigid, spastic, hands splaying, his neck, sometimes his whole back arching backwards, a raw, splitting bow. Dolores "talked" using subtle eye movements or mucus-tinged sounds, the meanings of which mostly escaped Iris, although Joe, whose own speech was labored and sometimes slurry, always knew what she wanted. In her big grocer green housecoat, Dolores reminded Iris of an old, worn potholder, square and limp. Before they'd left Park Haven that morning, she'd helped her on and off the toilet, changing the sanitary pad, soaked dark red, that someone else had put on backwards and upside down.

Where's my old lady? Joe rolled his body over and over across the sand, until, on his back, he was looking boldly up Dolores's parted legs. On all fours, he crept around her wheelchair, swinging his head as if stalking prey, before nibbling at one of her puffy white ankles. Dolores grinned until drool fell from both sides of her mouth. Iris reached up with the edge of a beach towel to wipe it away.

Come on, buddy, let's hit the waves. Cradling Joe in his arms, Kellen smiled down at Iris. Cool shades, Iris.

All the better to hide, she thought. I don't want God's perfect likeness seeing me, damn it. She turned away and spoke to Dolores.

You OK, hon? Want anything from the van? A blanket? Another towel? You warm enough?

Dolores made a garbling sound Iris decided meant she was fine.

Look Dolores. Far out. Joe's got Kellen carrying him like a sack of potatoes straight into the sea. I'm going to run down there and find some shells for you. Be right back.

After a minute or so in the water, Joe's skin was marbled from cold, his teeth smacking together, so Iris and Kellen worked fast to get him up to the van in the parking lot. They went back to get Dolores, whose hat had blown off and gone pinwheeling down the beach. In her shirt pocket, Iris had a sand dollar, black mussels shiny as beetles' backs, even a channeled whelk to put in Dolores's room, on her dresser. Dolores shared a room with LaVerne who sat in bed watching cartoons, shouting the same phrases over and over—Good Dad, Good Dad, Good Dad, or Poddy Momma, Poddy Momma. Echolalia, one of the staff nurses called it. LaVerne could repeat a phrase for hours on end. A thing like echolalia would drive Iris out of her mind. LaVerne's half of the room was loaded with religious objects, calendars, needlework sayings (*Be still and know I am God*), crosses wrapped with plastic flowers. Dolores had a different worship going on her side. Beatles poster, Beatles figurines, biographies, paperweights, even a Yellow Submarine wall clock.

The four of them settled into the van, the heater roaring out uneven patches of heat. Kellen, who had started a conversation, was in the driver's seat, Joe beside him. Iris and Dolores were in the back. A double date, thought Iris.

Joe, I'm serious, man. Do you maybe want to take Dolores to a nice restaurant? How about the zoo? A movie? The Museum of Natural History? I'm pretty sure we can get the van whenever we want. What would you like to do next time?

Joe was bundled up in three beach towels; his face, splotched and red, poked out like a hatchet.

Get it on with my old lady.

What? Kellen looked blank.

Screw our brains out.

Dolores let out an insane giggle, a goosey shriek.

Dolores knows what I mean. At Park, it's a whole lot easier on them if we have no feelings. Of the sexual type. They keep the men and women separated. It's discrimination.

Kellen turned around. That so, Dolores?

She made a sound Iris easily interpreted as yes. With all Joe's horsing around, Iris had never once imagined them having sex. Fucking. How would they? Why would they want to?

Kellen was looking at her, waiting for help.

A motel? She said it so fast it sounded sleazy. It made her think of Evan's pornography.

Exactly. This is what, Saturday? I'll tell Mrs. Whoosit, the lady at the front desk, that the four of us are going to dinner Monday night, maybe a movie. Instead, we'll go to a motel.

An orgy? Joe's wet hair spiked out in black tufts from his beach towel as he head-butted the dashboard. Iris imagined plugging Joe and Dolores together, the way she used to mate her stuffed animals, wrapping plush arms around each other, pressing noses to kiss. Later, when she sat with Kellen on the steps outside the theater, waiting for Marcia and Howard, Kellen told her what Joe had said—Dolores had such a crush on her physical therapist in New York, that she'd had orgasms in her dreams, though she didn't know what orgasms were and Joe had to tell her.

You mean got to tell her. Joe would love explaining that. Do you think they're virgins?

What else, given where they live. Treated like they're spayed.

I feel dumb.

Why?

I guess I kind of thought of them that way. Spayed. That's how I thought of them.

Iris. How many people do you really know with cerebral palsy?

Two. Joe and Dolores.

So how much could either one of us possibly know about it? Hey, Joe says he's got quite a stash of pornography. He's been obsessed with sex for years now.

Lucky Dolores. Iris wondered if any of it came from Evan's Dirty Bookstore.

OK if I use this washcloth? Look at this shit, will you? I've had it ages. I can't believe I actually used to wear this crapola. Argh. Here's my old eyelash curler, we'll skip that, tweezers, skip those too. Here's something possibly useful—lipsticks, mascara. Want music, Dolores? Iris flipped the radio on, hoping it was OK with LaVerne, strapped into bed wearing an old football jersey and men's pajama bottoms, her eyes shut as if she were asleep. Iris plunked on the edge of the bed, her feet hooking for stability into the wheelchair spokes, and circled Dolores's face with the damp washcloth. She put the makeup on, brushed out Dolores's sparse ponytail, turned and reached into her backpack. I picked this up (she did not say steal, who knew Dolores's morals?) in a head shop on State Street, it's got these little mirrors sewn into the fabric—cool, huh?—it's from India. Iris rolled the red scarf, knotted it around Dolores's forehead. Okey-doke. Whoops, almost forgot the patchouli. *Très* seductive stuff. After splotching oil behind Dolores's ears, Iris reached into her backpack and dragged out a velvet dress, tie-dyed green and deep blue with long, polleny streaks of yellow. As Iris helped put the dress on, right arm first, head, then left arm, Dolores made an unmistakable moan of pleasure.

With the velvet bunched up so it wouldn't drag under the wheels, Dolores used her feet, the way she always did, to push her wheelchair toward Joe, waiting with Kellen by the front door. As she got close, he started rocking his orange wheelchair, pounding his fists on the padded arms. He had showered, his black hair was still damp, a bit of bloodied white tissue stuck to his freshly shaved chin. He wore jeans and a work shirt. Kellen's. He had a blue suede headband on. Kellen's.

Creep, Dolores managed to say. Her fake tortoise glasses were Scotch-taped on one side, the one small blight on her face, thought Iris.

There were two queen-sized beds, each with a thin, coral bedspread. All four of them stared at the cheaply framed pictures over each bed, one a velvet paint-by-number of a dark-skinned girl in a provocative, off-the-shoulder blouse, the other an ocean sunset with a seagull, (housefly, Joe said), battering across a permanently aggrieved horizon.

Motel art, said Kellen, causing Dolores to pitch forward with laughter.

Wine, shouted Joe. Kellen uncorked the bottle, poured wine into four plastic cups while Iris fussed, switching on the two bedside lamps, turning off the harsh overhead light, drawing shut the yellow, plastic-lined drapes, turning on the heater, and, mostly from habit, sticking two ashtrays and a wrapped soap bar into her purse. Then she sat by Dolores, poked a straw into her mouth, held the cup. Joe angled his head down to the cup on the nightstand and sucked noisily from his straw. Hold your horses, Kellen laughed. Don't go getting blasted.

Blasted! shouted Joe, kicking at the nightstand. Iris worried he got too excited. What if he had a fit, didn't he have those sometimes? And with Dolores so torpid, you worried the other direction, that she might quit breathing.

Iris poured herself another glass of wine. Maybe she should be the one getting blasted. This place smells like a head shop, she said. It's the patchouli. She waved her cup. Hurrah!

Dolores wants a separate bed. Joe's head was jerking to one side, his neck winging back, the bit of Kleenex still stuck to his chin.

Kellen looked perplexed. Who's sleeping?

Dolores hit her hand against her chest, rocked around and around in a small, tight circle. Oh, thought Iris. Nervous. They're both virgins.

She rolled Dolores into the green-tiled bathroom to pee. Afterward, when Kellen took Joe into the bathroom, Iris helped Dolores into the bed furthest from the door, where she lay face-up in Iris' dress, arms stiff along her sides, eyes blinking.

You look great, Dolores. Actually, she looked ready to cry. Iris picked the glasses off, set them on the nightstand. What's to see? Want help with the dress? Yes? OK. Arms up. Ally-oop. Iris unhooked the dingy bra, slipped it off Dolores's breasts, which were big-nippled and creamy, with wavy flags of hair, like seaweed, under Dolores's arms. Underwear too? The works?

Just then the bathroom door crashed open. Joe sailed out in his wheelchair, naked, except for Kellen's blue headband. *Do-lo-reys...* he sang out. *Do-lo-reys...* Before she could look away, Iris saw his erection, like a long white piano key.

Under the coral covers, Dolores rolled her body in a low wave.

With the windows of the van cranked down, Iris and Kellen sat awhile, unsure what to do. Iris stared at the neon-blue sign, Sea Breeze

Motel, making new words out of the letters. SEAR, BREAST, TOE, TEAM, BRAT.

Hungry, Iris?

No, but I keep picturing one of them, both of them, falling out of bed.

I'm worried about the wine. Joe was pretty hammered.

No, the wine was great, it made them both feel really adult. Me, too.

Wine made you feel adult?

Just kidding. I don't know what I'm saying. What time is it?

Joe asked for two hours, right? Wow. An hour and fifty minutes to go.

Hey, Kellen. What did you say during yesterday's rehearsal—about dialogue?

I said dialogue is the last thing that happens between two people. That's not original by the way. I read it somewhere.

That's OK. It's still true. Everything happens before we speak.

They walked, not far from the motel, down a sandy embankment swollen thick with spears of ice plant, until they came to a railroad track, its rails like wet, pitted lines of silver. There were trees, tamarisks, along either side, and a cool wind blew off the ocean as Kellen and Iris balanced on opposite rails, one foot ahead of the other, heel-toe, heel-toe, arms outstretched, keeping even with each other. When they came to a clearing beyond the trees, Kellen ran easily up a steep, rocky slope and stood facing the sea. Iris stepped off the rail, anxious about her heart, though she knew her heart was perfectly fine. Catching her breath, looking up at him, she saw something she would try, later, to draw in her journal before ripping out the page. She would sketch a tall young man standing on a sandy bluff overlooking the sea, a poet-prince, his long brown hair buffeting around his shoulders. She could not capture the dangerous purity, the ominous innocence, standing as if on an otherworldly threshold, something she would later see as a premonition she had denied. Just as her heart hurt from the sight of him, Kellen turned and called down to her, held out his hand to bring her up the last shifting steps to the hilltop with its inky tussocks of beach grass. They faced the sea, her hand caught in his, in the simplest way.

Two hours later, when there was no response to Iris's gentle knock, Kellen turned the motel key. They found Dolores and Joe on the floor between the two beds, in a tangle of blankets, asleep in each other's arms.

Since Kellen was over an hour late, Marcia, like the pick-up-the-pieces wife in Joe Egg suggested they just do a line run-through. Iris repeated the one thing she knew, that Kellen was supposed to have been back from Los Angeles where he'd gone to visit his mother. The four of them sat on the black painted floor of the stage, ditching their accents, even Howard, who had a pawky head cold and kept honking into his monogrammed handkerchief. Audrey was sulking, so Marcia gave her Kellen's part, a mistake as this involved a three page monologue which Audrey trawled through with dogged apathy. When the offstage phone rang, Howard leapt at the excuse to exit such misery, then came back with ridiculous news, something about a kid in a Corvette running a stop light at seventy miles an hour, hitting Kellen's green Volkswagen.

She walked around the north wing of Park Haven, guessed which window, raised the sash, stuck her head in.
Joe? Can I come in? It's me.
He was there, in the dark. Stigler's bed was empty. A radio was playing.
Sure. Kellen with you?
She could not say. Not yet. Hey, Joey. Let me get into bed with you a minute, would you?
The need to be held, the hunger to be naked. Iris took her dress off, the green and blue one, slipped off her sandles, her underpants.
She held his skinny, stiff, trembling body. He told her about that night with Dolores, how she let him touch her, then got afraid so they started laughing, rolled off the bed, fell asleep holding each other. Dolores and I were kind of hoping you and Kellen could take us to that place again. That motel? You should see. Dolores craves me now. She's all over me.
Iris felt his erection against her thigh. She ran her hands along his arms, his chest, reaching up to his face, his hair, her fingers touching the blue headband.
It's all right, she said, moving a little, putting him inside her. This is good. And Kellen's here.

Dolores too?

Yes. Which made her see all three of them in some blue, choppy movie, one bed for Joe and Dolores, one just for Iris. After he cried out, coming inside her, she rested her head on his white, racing chest and heard something like pain, the roaring of the sea.

"No doctors," he says. "I know what they'll do. They'll shove me through all their neato machines!" He says it like that, like a punch line. "Ha! No. No way. Ha!" I've imagined the dark mental screening room in Martin's head, with its wry, blinking audience of other Martins in seat rows, each with their auburn hair parted perfectly on the side. There's a grim nervousness in there, too. You hear it throughout Martin, seismic tremors far beneath Movie Land, making all the sulky Martins restless in their seats.
    (Broun, page 111)

But the Fifties Really Take Me Home

Edward Mycue

I was born in the Depression nineteen thirties.
We left Niagara Falls in (in a forty-six Ford)
nineteen forty-eight and drove to Dallas.
I was eleven and in sixth grade in Our Lady
of Perpetual Help where Sister Mary Catherine
was principal and Father Burns, then Father
McCoey, then Monsignor Faletti, was priest.
Sister Mary Nolaska was my teacher and Luther
Bartlett, Walter MacAdams, Mary Pasternak and
Patsy Biasatti were some of my greatest pals.
No, it was Esther Biasatti and Patsy Van Winkle.
Patsy's little brother in my sister Margo's
class was properly named Mister Van Winkle be-
cause their day-proud, Arkansas dad declared
that by God they're going to call my son "Mister."
I graduated eighth grade in nineteen fifty-one
and off we went, my best buddies, Frank
Knickerbocker & me, to N.R. Crozier Technical High
right in the center of Dallas on Bryan Street
where from my homeroom window I saw the Republic
National Bank grow to its aluminum fifty floors.
There Dixie Dueth was the first president of
the first Elvis Presley fan club, claim to fame.
And classmate Trini Lopez had his homegrown band.
Tech's "Wolves" had silver and maroon colors.
Years come, go, but the fifties take me home.

OPEN CITY

> You sit in your room.
> Three cigarettes
> buy you
> the dawn.
>
> (Bakowski, page 95)

Clara

Joanna Kirk

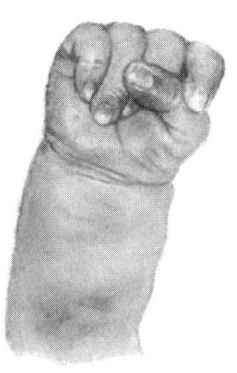

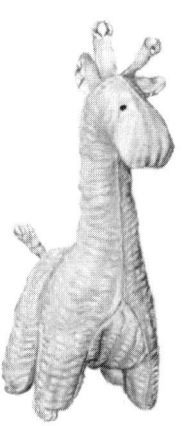

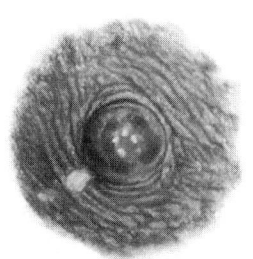

OPEN CITY

> Any minute now I expect Patrice to give me an ultimatum. She has a pun for this, too. Ultimatum becomes old tomatoes, as in, "They've been living together for five years, so Marcy finally gave Jack the old tomatoes: marry her or move out."
>
> (McNally, page 125)

Places

Harvey Shapiro

The Pazzi Chapel in Florence
and the Mosque of the Golden Dome
in Jerusalem and Cynthia's cunt
have been the loci of my strongest
aesthetic experiences—overwhelming
solitude and an unearthly light.

Epitaphs

Harvey Shapiro

I bought an outmoded plot
early in life about a Poet
and his Muse, both
characters now defunct.
For a while, it was like living
in an opera. Now it's not.

The drama has gone out of
the Long Island Expressway.

A man can't fight everything
that comes through the door,
I said to Death.

Cape Anne

Harvey Shapiro

A bee working over the roses
abutting the white porch
where I sit shaded,
two gazebos before me, beyond
them the soul-immersing sea.
In my dream last night
Robert Lowell came to me
weeping great tears. He
sat across from me, his
body hunched. Someone had passed
bitter judgement on his work,
and I, who hardly knew him
in life, had to comfort him
in death, while my own wreckage,
sun-struck, gleamed in the shallows.

Confusion at the Wheel

Harvey Shapiro

To the broad blue sheet of Biscayne Bay
where the dead parents commingle
and maybe their last prayers for the children
still stain the lucent surface
I returned at an age older than my father's.
I am older than my father
I said to the cruising pelicans,
to the lotus eaters, to the junkies
lurking in the pink and yellow
deco palaces of Ocean Drive,
in South Beach, Miami. Miami.
Moon over Miami. You can't die in Brooklyn,
my younger son said to me years ago,
you have to die in Miami.
I hear the waves ramping along the shore
by the dessicated palm trees,
and I think, this ocean,
this sea of time but without past,
without future, featureless, sans shape,
is my true home. Chaos is my home
and these family nostalgias,
this Miami vice, only
a quick trip to normalcy.
I remember Donald Barthelme's fable
about his real-dead father,
and Dylan Thomas's fierce father,
and my own father, confusion at the wheel.

Überfremdung

Sébastien de Ganay

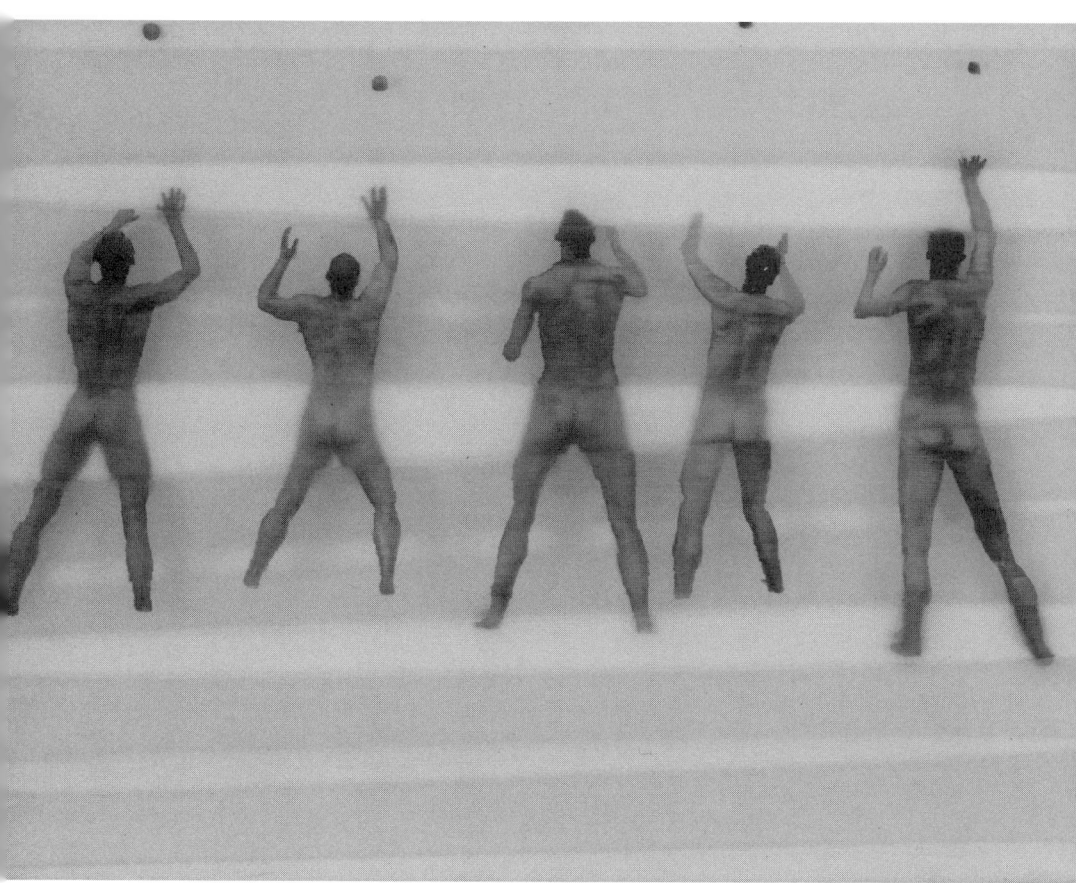

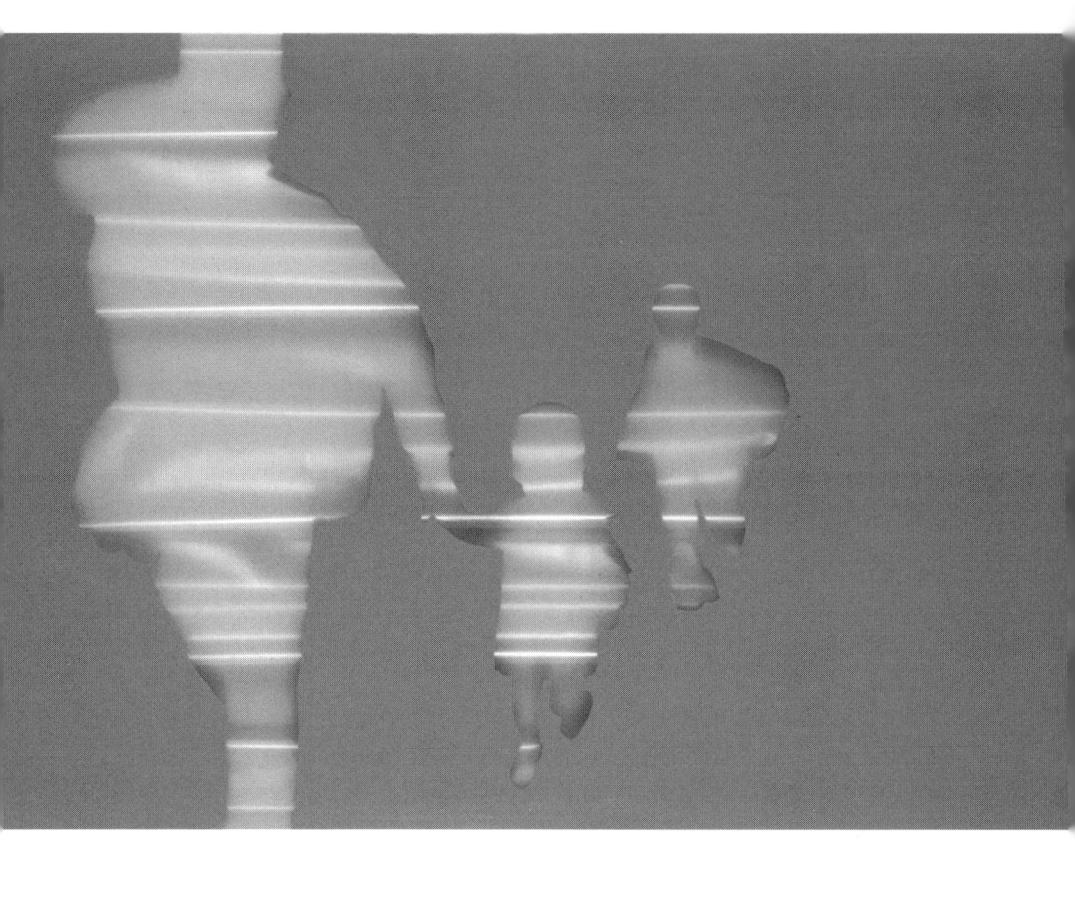

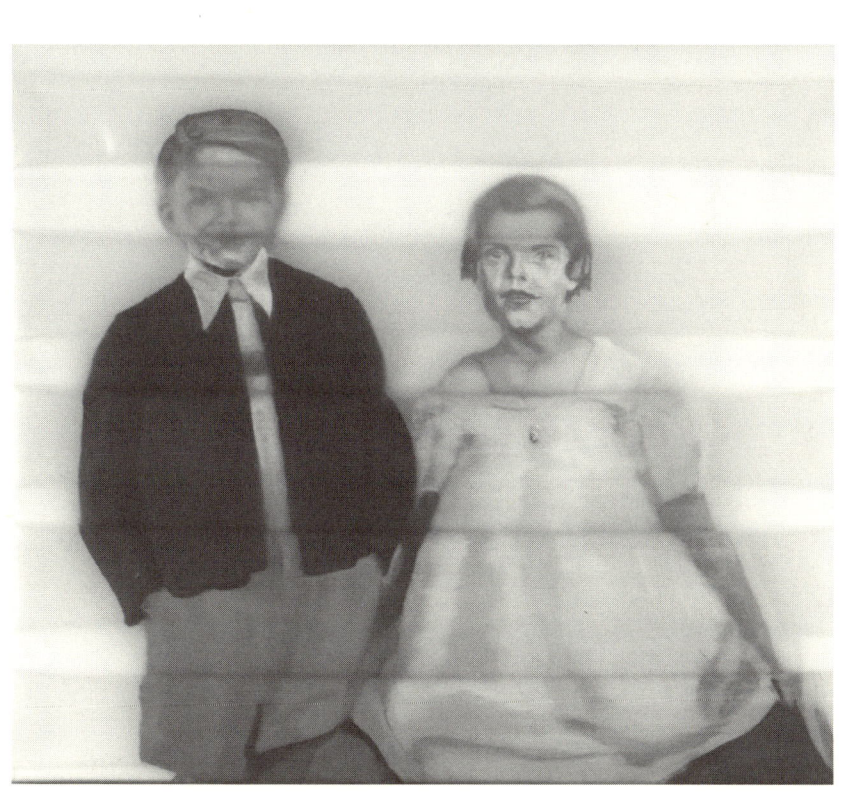

OPEN CITY

On the Cliff

Gregor von Rezzori

AMONG THE DREAMS THAT HAUNT ME, THERE IS ONE, MORE persistent and tormenting than others, which conceals that which represents—if I am to express it in literary terms—"the unfathomable mystery of my being." The dream proceeds in an unquiet flow, interrupted by blank periods of unconsciousness and by raggedy specters, yet draws on with an inexorability which fills me with terror. The logic of its images is deceiving. It holds true only for as long as I let myself drift in its flow. When I watch this dream from within itself, as, so to speak, from a diving bell, the images drift by me like so much flotsam carried by an inundation. There is no apparent significance to be found in them, even though, in their original context, they are sure to make sense, just as in the waters of a flood, the drifting bird cage with the dead bird, the face of the grandfather clock without hands, and the floating dresser drawer, in which a cat has sought refuge, gain a connective meaning when these diverse items are understood as parts of the house in which all of them originated. There exists a similarly unifying concept for the images of my dream. It may be called "I" and in its totality it represents an aggregate of individual character traits. But this "I" is not the tenant of the flooded house, even though I know with the certitude of the dreamer that whatever I experience relates to something I cannot name, but which constitutes the core of that concept of "I" and, thus, the core of myself. This, incidentally, is a thoroughly malevolent core: It is the origin of the flood which destroyed the house. Although this is to be understood merely in all the ambiguity which epitomizes the state of dreaming. In it, images are experienced and experiences are imagined. Metaphors flow into one another in a semantics of meanings all their own. But what they signify to me is unambiguous: my "I," in reality, does not exist. It is an abstract concept. Alike, in the realm of geometry, a point through which an infinity of lines are running and which by itself, nevertheless, is without dimension. It is the vanishing point of a cyclopic vision, a one-eyed perspective, in which all that is happening is gathered up in an existential experience of beingness. It is exclusively my own and yet I cannot define it by the declaration: "This is I!"

I was about to prepare my dinner: roasted calf's heart. I was hungry after an overcast day spent in a brown mood. I'm alone in my house. My servant—attendant, gardener, companion in solitude, call him what you wish (he, too, is now alone since the woman with whom he entered my service has left him), after having finished with his chores (whatever these may be; they are not of my concern), probably sits in dull apathy in front of the TV screen in the improved barn where he lives. We hardly exchange more than three words in a week. This morning he brought me from the village butcher some calf's heart for the dogs, still warm, for Monday is slaughtering day. I fed the dogs the cartilaginous, fatty ventricles and reserved some of the tender pieces for myself. I love to eat heart. Quickly broiled with a little butter, flavored with a bit of pepper and nutmeg, it is more succulent, heftier, and "heartier" than any other kind of meat.

The dogs, too, are wild for it. The greed with which they wolf down the pieces is frightening. They are heavy-set Neapolitan mastiffs, mouse-gray with broad white chests and enormous dark-gray heads, reputed to be highly dangerous. I have been warned repeatedly not to feed them by hand. I did it all the same today, even though my fear of them makes the hair at the nape of my neck tingle. On the butcher block where I always cut my meat, the points of the heart lay in front of me, plump and rosy, with delicate purple veining beneath the silkily shiny skin, that already had begun to dry out: sharply dissected, malignantly inflamed and swollen glands.

I understand why the women with whom I lived in the end all abhorred me. I used to suffer from an all-consuming paranoia. Time and again I was caught up in the manic concern that I had caught one of those venereal diseases, of which, during my childhood and adolescence, I had been given graphic descriptions to rival medieval presentations of hell. Their coloring was the same as that of altar panels of the Sienese school: the fiery red of festerings, the livid green of pus, the yellowish liquefaction of decomposition. When these came to haunt me, I lost all reason. The slightest reddening of my penis would send me into ludicrous frenzies. I could not keep myself from checking several times daily whether the pure cyclamen-shaded silkiness had not been marred by a small, hard, raspberry-colored primary symptom, which soon would proliferate into fearsome sores; or whether from the slit of my urethra that, with its slightly protruding opening formed a kind of thin-lipped mouth which showed an embarrassing resemblance to the mouth of my mother, was not issuing the mealy drip of an ever more corrosive flow which would dissolve my testicles. Obsessed by such fantasies, I inspected the part of my body in which my sense of selfness was concentrated even more intimately than in any other, such as, for instance, my hand, that obedient and devoted servant, indeed my most humble one, without which I would be nothing and even would be unable to make a living. (For I am by profession a woodcarver of sacral figures and not a bad one: my sculptures of the Madonna are displayed in some of the most prestigious art galleries.) In this, my hand, myself is much more concentrated than in whatever is inside my skull, where allegedly all originates that elevates life above the dumbness of sheer animal existence. (While, in fact, nothing grander takes place there than a succession of surrealist images, not unlike those in my nocturnal dreams.)

At first, women usually were amused by my eccentric obsession. A sprightly creature, whom I had picked up out of a tour bus when I was still living at the seashore above a cliff and who then stayed with me for some weeks, always participated with diligence in my self-inspections. She was a puckish thing, graceful and lively, full of droll fancies and always cheerful. I would have every reason to be grateful to her. She helped me to get over a difficult time, when I lost all my hair. This happened so unexpectedly and with such thoroughness that, at first, I was as if spellbound by the process itself and hardly considered to what an extent if transformed my whole appearance. One morning, as I was combing, I suddenly held whole tufts of hair in my hand. As I wiped my face with a washcloth, I rubbed away my eyebrows. I no longer had to shave. My pubic hair disappeared; my chest and my armpits, my arms and my legs became as smooth as those of a child. Soon, my head, too, was totally bald and of a silky sheen, flushing to roseate pink under the weakest rays of the sun. It was fascinating. But then, when several physicians told me that there was no known remedy against this loss of hair, that one knew nothing of its causes and could only surmise that those were psychosomatic in their origin, so that I had to conclude that I would remain a freak for the rest of my life, a bleak albino, a livid worm, only then did I really get panicky. The girl, her name was Lisa—incidentally, the same name as that of the girl to whom, as common parlance has it, I had lost my innocence—this the second Lisa in my sexual career; this girl, then, in the most disingenuous and natural way prevented my ending up in an insane asylum. She not only took the liveliest interest in my sporadic inspections of my penis, but also in the rapid progression of my baldness. She said I now looked altogether like a penis in full erection, since my glabrous head in its taut plumpness resembled nothing so much than a hardened glans.

She was witty and without prejudices. Once I told her the story of the maid, her namesake Lisa. She was the daughter of Furlan peasants, with whom I, a naïve and readily aroused adolescent, used to wrestle as with my schoolmates, until one warm Sunday afternoon, when my mother happened to be out of the house and our scuffling in her room got out of hand, ended up in another activity, which left us both, still panting and not fully realizing yet what had happened, with a dull feeling of guilt and a vague repugnance and disgust for each other. The change in our reciprocal behavior, so totally different from that day onward, when previously we had dealt with each other almost like siblings, aroused the suspicion of my mother. She dismissed the girl and then, to test the reaction this would provoke in me, told me that she had to let Lisa go because this supposedly innocent country child had contracted a venereal disease.

I managed to appear unconcerned. But in reality, my fear was horrifying. Even though I knew it to be a calumny, merely a trick of my mother's to find out how far I had gone with this girl; the latter herself might not even have known that she had been infected. Although she kept herself very clean, she hadn't been a virgin. And who is to know the type of men with whom a maid knocks about on her days off. I hated my mother. I hated her anyway, but now I hated her all the more for the low cunning of her ruse, with which she had tried to entrap me. I went about with murderous thoughts; I was a mere sixteen. I would have been capable of an act of violence, if I had found only the slightest sign of an infection on me and, without rhyme or reason, would have held my mother responsible for it. The aversion that filled me when I thought of what had happened in the maid's room, the bestial, obsessive, despicable coupling of the sweating bodies in the messed up, crumpled clothing, exposing only the genitals, the sliminess of the secretions, the disheveled bed linen, which had not been freshly changed for God knows how long and from which emanated an obtrusively female odor, the sticky, loose hair of the maid, her hot, bloated face, distorted by lust—all flowed together in the loathing I felt for my mother.

My mother was reputed to be very beautiful, in spite of her thin lips; someone once remarked that she drove men crazy with her hangman's smile. Even today it is only with distaste that I recall the overblown rifeness of her femininity, her glorying in the role of the arch-female, in which she saw herself and as which she found herself confirmed by everybody around her; it is only with intense repugnance that I remember the strong smell of her hair, which was her constant preoccupation and which Lisa had to brush and pin up mornings and nights, so that hairpins would be lying all over the house and I would find them between the pages of books and on the breakfast table; even the entrance hall was pervaded with the smell of that blonde mane, which my mother wore towering on her head. It drove me to insanity to see the men who came to visit us—those suitors with the comportment of lounge lizards, whom my mother called "admirers"—dilate their nostrils in the effort of catching a whiff of her "female effluvium." I knew that my mother was—as the saying has it—as cold as a fish, incapable of any affection, let alone of any tenderness. It was said that she had driven my father to an early death; I had never known him. Her suitors she kept on a string, and, in my own belief, none of them actually were her lovers. I would have been aware of it, for such things cannot remain concealed in a middle-class apartment one shares together.

What I clearly remember is that an aura of sexuality always surrounded the female whom I'm obliged to call my mother. She led an indolent life, but raised me with Spartan harshness. The only proof of affection I ever got from her was the permission, later the command, to join her in bed during her after-lunch siesta. As long as I was a child, I derived a certain pleasure from this, although even then I avoided touching her overly smooth, heavily scented skin or even her underwear. But the bed was large, warm, and soft, it was the matrimonial bed of my parents and the only place of voluptuous safeness I knew at the time. Yet, all too soon it also became a source of disturbing emotions. She lay there almost naked, merely covered by a thin silk robe under which I imagined her heavy breasts held by a bra. Soon other parts of her body crowded my imagination. I felt sick when thinking of those other carnalities: the slick belly with the indented navel and its swelling out to the edge of the brief panties, which she presumably wore and which I fancied to be so tight as to define clearly the mound of her pubic hair underneath. She made little effort to hide her corporeality and, at home and during most of the day, went around in nothing but her thin dressing gown, unless she—as she termed it—"dressed to kill." In our small provincial town, she was thought of as always being in the height of fashion. In the secret of my own heart, I called her a slut.

During puberty and even more so in its aftermath, this sultry siesta hour, next to a woman I loathed, caused me intense anguish. With that lust for domination peculiar to her, my mother had known how to shape this ritual togetherness into a duty I owed her. I sweated next to her. Needless to say, I couldn't sleep. The thought of what my schoolmates—I had no real friends—would say, if they knew that each day, during the best leisure time, I was ordered into the bed of my mother, made me blush all over. What bothered me most was that I was unable to prevent certain effects on my awakening virility. Hard as I tried, I could not constrain the surge of my blood. It got so that the thought alone of that siesta produced an erection with me. I was strongly developed and my pubic hair was precociously full. The idea that my mother could consider or, even worse, might actually become aware of my condition, brought me to the verge of despair. Had it happened—or rather, had she betrayed in any way that such had occurred—I would have killed one of us, her or myself. Meanwhile, however, I had to continue fulfilling my daily postprandial duty of our shared siesta. Nor was I exempted from it after the affair with the maid.

Lisa—not the maid, but that person with whom I lived years later and not so long ago in that house on the cliff above the sea—Lisa happened to be the only human being with whom I ever spoke of that episode. Not so much because I might have set any special trust in her; rather I believe it was the shock over the loss of my hair that made me confide in her. She had the gift of making light of everything, without taking anything lightly. At times, she reminded me of a tightrope walker I had seen at the circus in my childhood: I saw her balancing a delicate Japanese umbrella above her silver wig, while her feet groped and glided forward on the rope, then tripping swiftly and lightly over its entire length. Nor did Lisa ever lose her equilibrium and poise while hearing my confessions. She listened to me, alert and with concerned attentiveness, and then said: "I thought of a good metaphor for expressionism: instead of speaking of primary symptoms having the color of raspberries, you should rather speak of raspberries having the color of primary symptoms." It had no connection whatever with what I had been telling her (I had not mentioned any primary symptoms, least of all any raspberry-colored ones; a disgusting idea!), and yet I felt relieved in a strange sort of cheerful way. Women are odd creatures indeed.

But let me get back to what I had started to recount: today, as the points of heart lay before me to be cut up, I suddenly was overcome by the feeling that once more I was back there, hovering above the cliff. I shall try to describe this more accurately: it is a kind of hatred, intensified to a celestial degree. It renders the world transparent to my eyes. I somehow feel that this hatred is part of God's essence, in which I share. At the same time, it crushes me down to the very depths of the humanly experienceable. If, at the beginning, I spoke of those images as being the flotsam of my life's story as it appears in my dreams, such seizures of divine hatred are the eddies in that flood. They pull me down to the bottom. Above them swirls the froth of my existence.

I was about to cut the meat. I take pleasure in cutting meat with very sharp knives, particularly heart, which is firmer and more elastic than other kinds of meat and which, under the blade, bursts open more satisfyingly, displaying so to speak more carnal cuts, from which only a few sparse drops of blood seep out. Before I start cutting, I sharpen the knives on the whetstone. I do this, sensuously taking my time, with a quick crossing of the blades in front of me, as I have learned to do it from butchers. I appreciate fine tools; my carving knives, my chisels and scaupers I also keep shiny and sharp. Wood is a responsive material, which I carve with a pleasure proportionate in its voluptuous intensity to the wood's degree of hardness. The case with meat is different and very special. The sinking in of the blade is an experience of erotic immediacy, albeit only if the knife is exceedingly sharp, for then one feels as if the meat actually were to open itself to the blade. Ordinary knives do not cut well. That's why I acquired a set of real butcher knives, from cleaver-like heavy ones, with which to hack apart bones, all the way to tiny ones, viciously curved, with which to peel, with short, hissing, strokes, the tendons from their enveloping sheaths.

But the local butcher here is an average man of no particular interest, who knows little of all that. Only his appearance is out of the ordinary. He is one of those blaze-faced redheads, who are frequent among Ashkenazi Jews, and whose skin is not merely freckled, but spotted and flaming like that of salamanders. They pinch their faces into a permanent grimace, as if they were squinting all the time into the heart of flames. Someone told me once that they are the descendants of the tribe of Juda, to which the mother of Christ belonged. For Jews, the ritual kosher slaughterer, the so-called *shochet*, is respected as someone holding almost priestly rank.

The slaughterer who advised me when buying my set of knives was not the local butcher, but the one in the village at the seashore, above which I lived on top of a cliff in a tiny white-washed house built of rocks and pieces of marble and made up of three rooms around a patio overgrown with bougainvilleas. The way I see it now, I was very free then, master of my own destiny, of greater zest, and experiencing my life much more intensely than now. This ended when my hair began to fall out. The butcher down in the village took as lively an interest in this phenomenon as the blithe creature, who was living with me at the time. I was probably the butcher's best customer and I treated him like a friend. In return, he favored me with his choice pieces of meat. He was a handsome man, not overly tall, but imposing in stature. His hair in front was getting sparse. I recall a pair of rather disturbing gray eyes, radially striped with lines of yellow, as the eyes of cats or goats. If one looked into them, the iris, nailed down by the black pin-point of the pupil, seemed to start whirling around it, as a wheel of fortune turns around its hub. The eyeballs were of that bluish white, peculiar to freshly peeled hard-boiled eggs. In my memory of him, I see those eyes above a blood-smeared, white linen apron. Those eyes rivet my own, while his hands, in a kind of autonomous and almost unconscious dexterity, continue to manipulate his knives. I admire any kind of craftsmanship and I am proud of my own skills. His hands were well-formed, strongly veined, with sensitive fingers and spatulate nails which, despite all the wallowing in blood, he kept spotlessly clean. The hands of an artist. What was most impressive were his arms: massive and muscular, powerful, as if fed by the constant handling of raw meat. The skin of the forearms was ivory matte and covered by a black, silken fleece; on the inner side, however, they were hairless and above the elbow of such smooth and swelling whiteness, as elsewhere one only finds in the breasts of comely women. All the movements of the arms and the handling and strokes of the knives were skillful and precise in their execution, irrespective of whether these served to heave a whole side of beef down to the cutting block from the murderously pointed, S-fashioned hooks, affixed to the ceiling of the store; or, with incredibly well-aimed hatchet strokes, to split open a joint; or separate ribs with broad, heavy blades; or peel crunchingly the red fleshy parts from their surrounding cushions of fat with short, dagger-like knives. I bought from him only the very best meat of young steers which, in addition to a few lambs, he slaughtered regularly each week. The village was tiny and, apart from myself, he didn't have many regular customers. He treated me as a privileged client. A kind of trusting relationship developed between us. Once, when he got into trouble, I was able to help him out. But of this, more later.

The place where this occurred was renowned for its beauty. Whether this is so still today, remains to be seen. Even then, swarms of tourists invaded it in summer, but kept to the beach, where heretofore only the huts of fishermen had stood, so that all too soon a rank proliferation of villas, hotels, dance halls, boutiques, espresso bars, and self-service stores began to form a new subdivision, climbing the slope of the hill to join the old *borgo*, whose houses were glued to the precipice like a colony of swallow nests. The hill itself rises sharp and abruptly from the flat shore to form a cape protruding into and towering over the sea. Since days of old, this striking formation was seen as a petrified giant reclining, his chin supported by his hand and gazing out at sea. Along his back and during my time, the olive groves still climbed unchallenged and unspoiled within rubble-walled retaining terraces all the way to the cork oak woods, which extended their stunted growth along the ridge of the hill. Nights, the thrushes sent their sweet strains, a succession of three simple notes, up to the heights of the star-blazing heavens. A road, hewn from the rock, winds its way in serpentines up to the ridge, and then turns into a stony path ending where the rocks, bare and vertiginous, drop down to the sea's foamy surf below. Barely a dozen steps from the abyss, on the highest point—the bald crown of the giant, if you so wish—there stood my house.

This hardly would have been a good place for someone who likes solid ground under his feet. But I myself, I'm rather inclined toward the opposite. The closeness of the heavens where I lived often made me think that I actually was floating up there. This greatly benefited my work; it was there that I carved some of my most inspired Madonnas. I led a secluded life. Once a week I went down to the village, took care of my mail and did my shopping, exchanged some commonplaces with the butcher, drank a coffee in the bar of the general store on the tiny village square, and once more withdrew to my airie up in cloud-cuckoo-land. I worked hard. Since my works sold like hotcakes in the souvenir shops, I had to produce them in series, but still carved all of them by hand. Yet, this was mechanical work. Whenever I created a prototype of my highly popular carvings of the Annunciation or of the even more widely sought-after Mater Dolorosa or Pietà, I avoided being influenced by models from Italian classical art. My inspiration came from nature herself.

The confined ground, on which stood my house, was barren. Wherever enough earth had accumulated in the rock fissures, caused by the incursions of cacti and thistles to allow for the growth of thyme, rosemary, and broom; the air was rich with their fragrance. From the dwarf pines, courageously holding their own in the lee of rocky projections, the chirring of the cicadas sawed at the shimmering heat of the afternoon. In the blue expanse, showing between the pale lilac blossoms of the wisteria hanging from the trellised pergola in front of the house and the dark green oily leaves of the laurels, that vast blueness showing between the buddings of the rosebays planted there in large earthen jugs, sky and sea barely could be distinguished from each other. Out there, at the merely suspected line of the horizon, floating in the silken smooth, mercurially mirroring sea, a sea, which in its rare moments of turmoil would take on purple shades, streaked with steel gray and flecked by whitecaps—out there I knew of an island. It could only be made out on days of fickle weather. But then it floated, hair-thin in its contours and transparent as a medusa, it floated out there as a heart-tugging promise between heaven and sea. It was difficult for me to believe in its concrete geographic existence, even though I knew that it was a section broken off ages ago from the immense rock mass on which I stood, evidence of some far-off geological cataclysm, a kind of longingly reiterated echo of the homing summons sent out by the maternal terra firma. It was a vision only rising sporadically from boundless infinity. Far, far off, remoteness faded to ever farther remove, and the opalescent mists, weaving in those far reaches, on most days deprived me of my island. On days of heightened air humidity, the delicate shadings changed from hour to hour, from purple to the palest azure and from bottle green to glassy turquoise sheerness, only to be swallowed up once again by the skies turning dull. Twice during the twenty-four hours of the sun's cycle, these hazy zones ignited and blazed with raging fires. A gradual nocturnal decomposition gave birth to sulphurous yellows, laboring in roseate pinks toward the flaming core and cutting a black, Ptolemaically flat disc out of the universe. Evenings, the reflection of these conflagrations played the gamut between orange and oxblood red, until it finally paled and once more coalesced into the darkness which had disintegrated in the morn. On stormy and cloudy days, a boiling and surging decay of all coloring took place, throwing the world through ever colder depths into the chaos from which once it had emerged. I experienced these dramatic transformations of color and light like the masterworks of our great German music. But the leitmotiv in all this was my island. In the immensity of the luminous skies, spreading their light prior to the shift in the weather, that island rose before my eyes as a pledge of hope, while I stood at the edge of the cliff, ready to reach it with a single step into nothingness. I happen to be entirely free of any feeling of vertigo.

This was not the case with Lisa, the person I picked up out of a group of tour bus passengers. I had seen her in the lower part of the village, at the bus station, where, just prior, I had delivered a carefully wrapped lot of my carvings for forwarding. The group was about to leave. The girl stood a little apart from her traveling companions, who were loading their luggage onto the bus, while she was gazing up at the cliff, as if taking sentimental leave from it. Half in passing I said, "Up there, that's where I live." I had heard the group speaking German and, therefore, spoke with confidence in what was the mother tongue of both of us. She did not falter in her upward gaze, but continued to look steadily at the face of the rock.

"Close to the drop?" she asked with some trepidation. I stopped next to her. She had whitish blonde, closely cropped hair, and, with her androgynously slim body, appeared younger than she was. As she turned her head toward me, I noticed on the bridge of her nose a spattering of pale freckles. She shook her head, as if trying to rid herself of a disquieting thought. "I get dizzy just thinking about it," she said. I knew her type of vacationers. They behave as if they were unfettered free spirits, but, in truth, are confined to the cage of their tight bourgeois prejudices.

To tempt her, I said, "Come up there with me. From the top you'll see so many fabulous things, that you'll get dizzy in a way quite different from the one you're imagining." She pointed to the bus, which was ready to leave. "What do you miss, if you get home a few days later?" I asked. "Nothing," she said to my surprise. She prepared to get her belongings from the bus. I was caught in my own trap.

She lived together with me on the cliff for several weeks. My distaste for much that is peculiar to women in no way lessens my urge to possess them. Nevertheless, I have to overcome a wave of contempt each time one of them yields to me. Lisa did so with an absentmindedness which betrayed that the particular man, who happened to penetrate her, mattered less than the circumstances under which this occurred. Even as we reached the house that first time, she clung to me and could not be persuaded to go closer to the precipice, be it only a step or two. When I myself approached it, to show her how perfectly safe it was, she called me back with a high-pitched plaintive cry and thrust herself under me. I took her in front of the threshold of my house. I had hoped to get rid of her again soon, but she was as if under a spell and it took days before she could will herself merely to walk around the outside of the house without my holding her hand.

Gregor von Rezzori

In spite of this, she did not want to leave. She was as if drunk with the sheer space, the blueness, the light. When my hair began to fall out, I had become so used to her that I no longer could imagine a time spent without her. I had lost my freedom, and for that I hated her.

Of all this I was reminded today when cutting the meat. I had severed off cleanly the points of the heart, dissected the ventricles and had thrown these to the dogs to feed on. The beasts caught them in midair, gobbled them down whole and were crowding me for more. These were four prime specimens of a heavy breed which, in times past, had been bred for bull hunts and for show fights with each other. Their mood could switch all of a sudden from pup-like playfulness to blindly raging aggression. When it got to their feeding, they stood for no nonsense. I knew that with respect to those pieces of meat on the butcher's block in front of them, they were of deadly determination. It is said that the sweat of someone who is frightened has a special odor, which is sensed immediately by dogs and prompts them to attack without fail. I felt fear. I felt it in my neck and in the pit of my stomach and, sickeningly, felt it issuing from my glands. I saw their flews dripping with saliva and how they already crouched to rush me. I was faster than they by a mere heartbeat: I took one of the points of heart and threw it far away from me in a wide arc. The dogs hurled themselves after it and all four reached their booty almost simultaneously. One could not make out which of them actually had snapped it up first; they had locked jaws in a savage tangle even before I could throw them the rest of the meat. It was a blood-curdling sight to watch them fight among themselves like pit bulldogs in some gruesome contest put on for show in some dark oriental harbor den. Their foaming and howling was hellish. Blood dripped from their gaping maws into the dust. I ran to the well, where a full bucket of water stood on its rim, and threw it at them. The cold stream hit the biting and growling brutes with such force, that they left off from each other. Even though fear still throbbed in my veins, I called each one separately in the most commanding voice I could muster and fed each of them one of the remaining apices. Each took his morsel in meek submission and no longer contested those given to the others. After having been fed, they licked each others' wounds, from which hung bloody flaps of skin. Then I went back into the house to change my shirt, which was drenched with the sweat of my fear. The triumph over the dogs had brought on in me a kind of elation, a "high" similar to the one I so often felt when living on top of the cliff.

Earlier, that house up there had belonged to a women painter, an eccentric person of Junoesque beauty and proportions, with raven-black hair in which a flower perennially provided a spot of color, as in those Tahitian women painted by Gauguin. But I saw her endowed rather with the long, fully turned limbs of Feuerbach's Greco-Bavarian goddesses, yet also with something of the somber fatefulness peculiar to the figure in Franz von Stuck's painting entitled *The Sin*. Among the people in the village, she enjoyed a certain respect, a mixture of awe, admiration and curiosity, on account of her unquestionable strangeness. Alone the fact that she had taken over the house on the brow of the cliff, directly above that vertiginous rock face, this dilapidated half-ruin, the remains, in all probability, of an old watchtower or lighthouse, itself perhaps erected on the foundation of some pagan temple from its marble splinters, from boulders and rocks, and the fact that she lived there, on the loftiest of heights, all by herself and in the most primitive manner imaginable, that alone already made her seem odd, almost weird. She only wore long black caftans, with sandals on her bare feet, so that the village children ran after her and called "Witch! Witch!" Her way of talking was equally bizarre. Her Italian sounded as if she had puzzled it together from words and idioms picked up at random, and she mixed it up in a happy-go-lucky way with homely interjections from her native German dialect, the one spoken in Upper Bavaria, having the broadness and earthiness of a flower-bedecked peasant cart. To the narrow minds in the *borgo*, she appeared shrouded in an aura of secrecy, even though the mysteries she might have concealed surely were of the most banal sort. She questioned the old women of the village about medicinal herbs; early in the morning, the fishermen saw her on the beach looking for shells; she never received any mail; and she mixed most of her paints from various kinds of earth and from plant juices. All this still could have passed. But she also rooted around for old inscriptions chiseled into stones and transferred these to sheets of papers, which she then glued together into long scrolls covered with cryptic, undecodable signs. The people in the mountains and the fishermen are highly superstitious. They charged her with practicing black magic. In addition, it was bruited about that she had illicit relations with various men in the village. Among those suspected also was the mayor, but the most prominent of those alleged lovers was the butcher with the gray eyes, even though they never were seen together, nor did she ever come to his store to buy meat. She was a strict vegetarian.

It would have been but natural for me to try to get to know her. Once the summer guests were gone, I was without women, for the girls of the *borgo* were unapproachable for foreigners. I shall not deny that the proud woman-painter captured my fantasies. In my mind, I passed in review the men who were alleged to have enjoyed her favors. The mayor was not to be considered seriously as a candidate: he was a wretch of a little man, with the bustling pomposity of the backwood politician. I could also exclude most of the other suspects, all of whom were henpecked and much too jealously watched by their respective wives. Only the butcher could be thought capable of meeting with her under cover of darkness in the surrounding woods or in the olive groves. He was a bachelor and, in contrast to all the others, he would not look puny next to her. Even though she was taller than he by almost a half a head, his massive arms were well fitted to handle and tame her in lust. In my imagination, I saw it like the coupling of a pair of giants. And for her, to be overpowered for once was bound to be blissful.

As to me, she discovered me when, one day, I had climbed up the hill, my mind full of all kinds of thoughts. It was the first time I was up there and I hardly noticed her house, let alone her presence. The vertical drop of the cliff drew me close. To test to what an extent I was free of vertigo, I stepped so close to the edge that the points of my shoes jutted out beyond it into the void. It was one of those days on which my island was visible. I looked at it for a long time. Then, when I looked down into the depths before me, I registered that I felt its tug merely as a barely noticeable pull in my testicles, yet sufficiently manifest to make me realize to what suicidal impulses this could lead if one were not entirely free of acrophobia. I turned around and saw the woman standing in front of the house, surrounded by cascades of wisteria blossoms. Her priestly robe was as black as her hair. "Oh my!" she exclaimed, *"Lei è il primo uomo che osa andare così vicino allo strapiombo."* I suppose that in remarking on my daring to go so close to the precipice she meant to flatter me, but I merely replied, "You can speak German to me. You know, I envy you this place. It's beautiful up here." She said, "Well, most men get a bellyache when they get up here and become aware of how close they are to the drop. The brick masons who helped me restore the house from the heap of rubble I found here, I practically had to tie them on with ropes. And I had to whitewash the house myself, for the *inbianchino* refused to climb up here." I wanted to ask her why she hadn't left it in its natural stone gray, since this would have made it less stark and more as if it had grown from the rock itself. But I forewent the question; I don't like to discuss the tastes of others. There are those who question the good taste of my own creations, presumably because they correspond to the most widely held predilections (which, incidentally, also happened to be the case with the works of Tielmann Riemenschneider). So I asked her instead: "And you? You don't get dizzy?"

Strangely enough, she didn't answer me. She examined me, silently and for some time, and then said, "I know you by sight from the village. You are a friend of the butcher." I nodded. "How long have you been here?" she asked. "This will be my third winter in a little while," I told her. "There's quite a while still before winter," she reflected. The blueness all around us was mesmerizing. Lizards scurried among the gravel around the house. Except for the chirring of the cicadas, not a sound could be heard. The breeze sweeping over the top of the hill was so light that it failed to move even the branches of broom and rosemary bushes growing in the lee of rock crannies, yet it wafted their aromatic fragrance over to us. The stone reflected the sharp light. Other than that, nothing was around us but blueness, blue the sky, blue the air, blue the sea: that airy, yet dense blueness of the South, a transparency reverberating in nothingness. "Will you have a glass of wine with me?" the woman in the black robe asked hospitably. It was only then, as she stepped into the house and out of the purple-blue cascade of the wisteria, that I noticed the flower in her hair.

Whenever I am with a woman for the first time, my urge needs to be strong enough to overcome my distaste for all the unappetizing and ludicrous aspects of sexual arousal. This did not happen in her case. Her beautiful, though majestically huge body steamed next to mine which, in comparison, seemed puny. Her arms were as thick as my thighs. It was obvious that she shunned the sun, for her skin was of that grainy whiteness, readily breaking out in sweat, typical of brunettes; her loose hair coiled on it like thick black snakes. She gasped at my side with closed eyes, a beauteous goddess awaiting my penetration of her flesh. I tried to climb on top of that gorgeous expanse of body, but my condition rendered vain any such effort. Mortified, I lay next to her. She opened her eyes, propped herself up on one elbow and looked down at me. Her breasts were heavy in their nakedness. The flower had fallen from her hair. With two fingers she took hold of my limp penis, held it upright and then contemptuously let it drop back between my thighs. Then she lay back in silence once more. Later, when my sexual instinct nevertheless had gained the upper hand over my phobia, she remained cold, much as I strived for her pleasure. As always when I have finished the labors of love, I jumped up to wash myself, but found no water. "There's an earthen jug with water in the kitchen," she said. "And, incidentally, I'm not poisonous." Much abashed, I left her. During the weeks that followed, I bought my meat at the other butcher in the lower end, the new part of the village.

It was unavoidable that we would meet again. Our fall into carnal sin—as I jokingly would term it later—was not repeated. Instead it had established between us a lasting and becalmed intimacy. Therewith our reciprocal relationship was settled once and for all. We had nothing to conceal or expect from each other. As a result, our differences of opinion, however sharply outspoken these were, also remained without consequences. I visited her fairly regularly in her house on the cliff. In its patio, well-protected from any wind, she had planted varicolored bougainvilleas, which had grown as sturdily as anything that sprouts up there from but a handful of earth under the blessing rays of the sun. It is there that I like to sit with her, drinking a glass of the dry wine of the region, for in the room which she used as her studio we inevitably started quarreling with each other. She was an abstract painter. And whatever she had to say about that was as confused a tangle as the color spatterings on her canvases. Nor did she want to listen to me, but stopped her ears with her fingers when I tried to tell her that art was in duty bound to find a language which is generally comprehensible and, thus, would act as a unifying force; that everything which we sense in art as being beautiful is expression of a striving and reaching for something unattainable, something beyond all artistic craftsmanship, a blossoming growing out of the fear of and the longing for God; that the obsession with the craft itself, unless restrained by that humbleness felt in the face of everlasting aesthetic canons, is bound to have a disintegrating effect, to become a ferment of decomposition, like the spirit that Houston Steward Chamberlain ascribed to the Jews; and that the blasphemous arrogance of the individual, the self-interpretation of the artist as liberating titan breaking the fetters of the world and investing it with new vistas, indeed was one of the most deplorable phenomena of an epoch already stigmatized by chaotic subversion and general moral decomposition.

It was obvious that in such arguments we also touched upon events in our more recent German past, even though we shied away from dealing with these more thoroughly, probably on account of the distaste for something already hashed through too often and yet not fully digested. And when she then rebuked me by asserting that my views were precisely those held by the type of persons most responsible of the chaotic decay of our times, I pointed out quite reasonably that disguise always was the devil's favorite artifice and that any truth can be perverted into serving a basic lie; yet I failed to convince her of the soundness of my reasoning. I then could bring to her attention merely the ironic fact that she, with all her innate, soil-derived natural powers, she, the daughter of peasants from Upper Bavaria, was committing a kind of biological treason by carrying on as the standard bearer of radical avant-garde ideas, a role which would have befitted me much better than her; my own father had been a professor of physics at one of the most prestigious German universities. The fact is that our opinions, our concepts, and our preferences diverged in every conceivable respect like day and night. In music, her liking was for Debussy and the twelve-tone composers, while my own preference was for Bach, Beethoven, and Brahms. As to Wagner, we knew better than to start a dispute on his account. Of course she made fun of my deep emotions stirred by the sight of those polychromatic symphonies accompanying the risings and settings of the sun which, from that peak between land and sea, could be viewed in so unparalleled a manner. But I was careful in keeping from her that what struck me most profoundly in those color effects attending the birth and death of the day was that these were precisely the shades of decomposition and of infernal damnation, and, at the same time those of my most intimate fears. Nor did I ever tell her about my island.

She frequently mentioned her intention of leaving this place.

"They'll bury it under concrete," she would say (meaning by "they" those anonymous forces of development directed against all that is natural and traditional, all that is close to the heart of the people, as if these forces were the outcome of some gigantic plot hatched by money-grubbing profiteers; nor did it help when I pointed out to her how contradictory such beliefs were to her lifestyle: despite all her avant-gardism, she was more conservative than I. Darkly she would prophesy, "Swarms of tourists will descend down here and they'll corrupt the youths of the village even more thoroughly than they are corrupted already by all those slick magazines, the radio, and the TV. Even before it'll come to that, I fear worse: an artists' colony will nestle here, you'll see. The place is just right for nuts fleeing civilization and seeking a pocket-size paradise. You and I will draw after us those of similar bent. For we, too, carry in us the curse of our species, the germs of a new breed, which we dislike as much as we dislike ourselves—becoming ourselves that ferment of decay, as you term it in accordance with the tenets of your high priest of racism." I refused to get entangled in such rhetorics. This was part of our constant mutual teasing and, in any case, was not to last much longer.

She stayed for another summer. Then, one day, the time had come. She told me that she had met an archaeologist, who wandered along the mountain ridges throughout Europe in search of the traces left by a mysterious prehistoric people. On his way, he had happened on her house and even had found among the stones around there some artifacts which proved valuable in his research. This legendary people—or rather this tribe—only had dwelled on heights from where any approaching danger could be discerned readily. In their migrations, these mountain nomads had left signs, meant probably as guideposts for those who followed. These objects were merely stones showing a natural resemblance with items from the everyday experience of Stone Age man, so that only very little handiwork was required to transform them into the things they were meant to represent: the heads of animals, for instance, or a skull, an embryo or a toad. These were findings of highest scientific significance and my friend, the painter, was so captivated by this undertaking that she decided to accompany the archaeologist in his quest. She had lived longer than enough in this place, she declared, and as beautiful and stirring as it was, she felt that it could inspire her no longer and that her creative impulses had began to stagnate. She proposed that I buy her house. The price was commensurate with such an unsellable piece of real estate. I gathered up my belongings from the guest house, where heretofore I had resided, and brought them up closer to the heavens by a few hundred yards.

Soon I realized that I could not have made a better choice. The house fitted my mode of life like a well-worn glove. I need say no more about its location, but the layout of the rooms also proved ideal. The largest of them, with the best light, served as my own studio as it had served the painter (though only after first cleaning off thoroughly all the spots and streaks of paint from the walls and the floor: as is the wont of some abstract artists, my predecessor had been in the habit of covering gigantic canvases with random squirts from the paint tubes). Across from the patio, on the westerly side, was the bedroom. The third room, connected with the other two by a narrow corridor, served both as kitchen and as living room. It only had the barest of furniture: a work table and a kitchen table, a bed and a few chairs. To make up for this bareness, there was a profusion of potted plants, some of them left by the painter and others that I had brought myself from below, all of them rankly luxuriating. There was no electricity, but I made do with candles and, in any case, went to bed so early, awakening before daybreak, that I hardly missed any artificial lighting. The only thing that was cumbersomely primitive was the water supply. It had to be hauled from a fairly distant source, located where the dirt road ended in a footpath. For that purpose, the painter had mounted a barrel on a wheelbarrow; it served me equally well. I had all I needed and lacked in nothing. I worked a great deal and I was happy in those days. All this ended with the arrival of the girl from the group of tourists.

Only once was my life perturbed prior to the appearance of Lisa. One day, after having lived for almost half a year in my aerie, the *carabinieri* came to call on me. For quite a long while they beat about the bush before finally coming out with their request: what had been my relationship with the woman painter, they wanted to know. Could I tell them something of her relations with other men? With the butcher, for instance? I told them the truth, to wit, that I only had scant information and that, too, merely by hearsay since, despite our occasional meetings, I had never gained any deeper insight into the private life of my predecessor in this house. But even as I was saying this, I felt—strangely enough—that I was lying, although I would not have been able to explain in what way, be it only to myself; in truth, I only said what I knew and what corresponded to the facts in the matter. It may be that the whole situation made me uneasy, ridiculous as this may sound. After all, I had a totally clean conscience—abstraction being made of my failing in the bed of the painter on the occasion of our first (and only) sexual encounter. That was the only thing I had concealed and that was hardly something to feel guilty about in the eyes of the authorities. Yet it may be that with the appearance of the representatives of law and order a basic, so to say generic feeling of guilt had been awakened in me, one that is innate and inculcated in all of us, at least in all of us Germans—but be that as it may, I was under the impression that my declarations sounded lame and that this did not escape the attention of the *carabinieri* who, as a consequence, invested their questioning increasingly with the character of a cross-examination. After they finally had left, my relief was such that only then did I become aware that I had forgotten to ask them the reason for their investigation. I was to learn a few days later in the village: The painter and the archaeologist both had been murdered.

It is by no means rare in Italy nowadays that a couple of lovers somewhere in a parked car, or campers on solitary beaches or in other remote places are being killed in cold blood. Robbery is hardly ever the motive. If the culprit is caught—which is the case rarely enough—the deed usually turns out to have been committed by a lunatic or by some fanatic decency apostle, determined not to tolerate any sexual act outside a properly darkened Catholic bedroom. Some are the acts of sexual perverts—if one does not include already among these the above mentioned champions of prudery. The painter and her archaeologist had been shot in their trailer not far from the village. It was said that in their search for antiquities, they had roamed for months over the ridges of most of the Italian mountain ranges, but had returned here for the winter because our own hill supposedly yielded the richest finds. The culprit could only be one of the locals. Thought the annual high tide of the tourist wave washed up innumerable foreigners on our shore, including some riffraff, it was still too early in the year for that, and the lonely olive grove, where the trailer had been parked, could only be reached by way of a lane so overgrown with brambles, wild vines and wood anemone as to be virtually impassable. The narrow terrace, where olive trees, neglected for decades, were writhing in catatonic contortions, suffocating in the clutch of creeper vines, was overshadowed by the oak and chestnut trees growing above, and shielded from view by the grove of poplars standing below; it was an ideal spot for a secret lovers' tryst. The ground belonged to the butcher.

The deed caused a great deal of gossiping in the village. I did not participate in it, but could not help overhearing the exchanges taking place in the espresso bar on the square. It was only then that I remembered an episode, which I had forgotten or, at any rate, and concealed from the *carabinieri*. One day, about a week prior to their inquiries, I had rolled the wheelbarrow with the barrel to the source, so as to fill it. As had also been the custom of the woman painter, I usually left this chore for the evenings, when the heat of the day had abated somewhat and the pushing of the full barrel up the slope to my house was less of a back-breaking labor. The shadow had lengthened and I was startled when suddenly a figure moved close by: from the bushes surrounding the source and the darkness of the cypresses, there emerged the butcher. We greeted each other, and he offered to wheel the water barrel for me up to my house. It wouldn't be the first time he did it, he said, albeit without explaining for whom he had rendered such a service—it would have been superfluous. I offered him a glass of wine, which we drank in the patio. Before leaving, he stopped on the threshold and took a pistol out of his pocket. "People say you're completely free of vertigo. Would you do me the favor of throwing this thing over the cliff into the sea? I found it not far from the source, probably left behind by the Germans, who operated an observation post up here during the war. There still are a lot of these dangerous toys lying around and God only knows what trouble they might cause if, perchance, some children were to find one of these things and play with it. I, for one, don't know what to do with it. I hate firearms and I am neither a hunter, nor am I much afraid of being attacked or robbed." He laughed. I took the pistol, went to the edge of the precipice and threw it out far enough, so that it fell into the sea where its waters were darkening into purple. "Satisfied?" I asked him. He gripped my hand and said "Thanks!"

It seemed obvious to me that a murderer wouldn't behave in that way. From the bar, I went over to the butcher's shop. We were alone; the housewives of the *borgo* bought their meat in the morning. "You've heard what happened to the painter, who owned my house before I took it over?" He nodded in silence. In front of his bloodspattered white apron, his skillful hands were sharpening a broad knife on the whetstone. Fascinated, I observed the play of his heavy arm muscles. "According to the police, it must have occurred the night before you came to my place," I said. His gray eyes were nailed into mine, while his hands mechanically continued to whet the blade. "The night after," he said. I nodded, "I just wanted to be sure. Just in case I might be questioned once more." Then I gave him my order for my weekly meat supply. This happened to be the day on which I went down to the new part of the village to mail a package with my carvings and, at the bus station, met the girl who was to witness my transformation into a glabrous grub worm.

Our being together started out quite pleasantly. I had no illusions as to her human worth. Nothing distinguished her from the great mass of her coevals belonging to the equalizing low level of postwar petit bourgeois society. She had attended decent schools and even had studied several semesters at a university, majoring in media science or some such new-fangled discipline. She had no job, at least not any permanent one, and I did not ask her how and with what she managed to provide for her life. She merely existed wherever she happened to be, and this appeared to be her sole and fulfilling vocation. She had no other purpose in life. On the strength of her perennial cheerfulness, she had developed this merely being-there into an asset: an airy, luminous presence, never annoying, never burdensome, always happy, fun-loving, unpretentious, and unobtrusive. Even her hysterical clutching at me whenever we came a bit close to the precipice did not bother me. Her fears at such moments reached erotic dimensions and I have to admit that I exploited this for my own pleasure. After having indulged in sexual acts until overtaken by sheer exhaustion, I only had to order her to imagine standing at the very edge of the cliff to drive her close to an orgasm and myself thereby into a state of renewed excitement.

I copulated with her without any restraint whatever. This is to be taken not only literally, but also in a twofold manner: on the one hand without the inhibitions I usually suffered when confronted with sexuality, and on the other hand without curbing any of my animal urges on grounds of aesthetic reasons (as, more that once in the past, I had despised myself for the crudeness of my rutting). With her, I let myself go. There was nothing in her of that which often made me shrink from all too ostensibly female women; her body was androgynous. With the exception of the pale stripe over her small breasts ("a bare two handfuls," she was wont to say) and the triangle at her crotch, which her bikini concealed from the rays of the sun, her skin was of the brown shade and also of the smooth texture peculiar to hazelnuts. She offered me her genitals—sparsely covered by a golden-blond fleece—and her other erogenous zones, as if severed from the seething, sweaty masses of flesh of the usual run of women, she offered them to me in a clean and—I am tempted to say—an almost aseptic way. Her vivacious sensuality left no doubt that she had had plenty of sexual experience prior to our own mating, yet I felt no fear in her case of inheriting some venereal infection from one of my predecessors. We checked this out with great thoroughness. She also put me at ease concerning everything else: she regularly took the pill; I did not have to exercise any caution. Though I regarded such reassurance as quite superfluous; I would not have had any scruples in impregnating her. Her body was not made for motherhood—or, more accurately, it precluded imagining her in that role. Nothing repulses me more in women than swollen bellies and heavy breasts. Certain paintings by Klimt bring home to me with such immediacy the horrors of the child carrying and birthing labors imposed on the human species that I find myself close to vomiting. This may seem to be in contradiction to the choice of my artistic subjects, for it is true that I carve almost exclusively the Madonna. However, I view her not as mother, but as virgin. As the bearer of a god, she is released from and beyond all sexuality and motherhood.

 Our idyll was not to last long. Sexual excesses not merely exhaust the body but, also and foremost, the soul. Soon I began to hate Lisa. Outside the sexual sphere, nothing bound us together. Our constant copulations soon took on the character of dumb animal monotony. At the same time I found myself in creative crisis. My faith in what I produced began to falter. I seemed to grasp all at once that this elf-like vaporously airy girl was playing with me an evil and arch-female game. My lack of vertigo on the cliff was bound to incite in her the bent towards destruction innate in all that is female. Her envy of my weightlessness drove her to arouse in me all of my basest animal instincts. She had to bring me back down to earth. I saw through all of this, but acquiesced in it. The situation had in it something mythically compelling. It was only with the greatest reluctance that I forced myself to work on the reproductions of my prototypes, the work which, after all, ensured my likelihood. Suddenly these seemed not merely banal, but in outright poor taste—kitsch, as the murdered painter had called it in her blunt way. And this deflected me from the convictions which, heretofore, had enabled me to maintain my artistic integrity. When I attempted to find, still always within the framework of my canons, a more severe artistic expression, one cleansed of sentimentality, I found myself getting close to those abstract forms I had rejected so vehemently in my argumentations with the dead painter. All this occurred so to say ineluctable and against my own intentions, almost as if my hands no longer were obeying my own will, but rather some command issued beyond freedom of choice. I need admit that this worried me not only because of considerations of an art-theoretical nature. My madonnas and crèches, my annunciations and pietàs had a very broad but specific market. The galleries, with which I worked, followed only very cautiously the direction in which the zeitgeist had been pointed by the giants of our period, such as Braque and Picasso, not to speak of the radical abstractionists, such as Mondrian and Kandinsky—a direction in which they were followed by most of the younger artists (albeit against their own true inclination, I am tempted to believe). I knew that if I were to follow suit, I would imperil my financial security. "You are right in staying put where you are." I heard the dead painter say. "You belong to the hide-bound, small-minded artistic middle class, and you work for the hide-bound, small-minded intellectual middle class, which always is lagging behind the times by a century."

She had not actually spoken these words while still alive, but she could have spoken them. I now talked with her ever more frequently; with Lisa, I could not talk of these problems. Presently—both for the benefit of the dead painter and my own—I began to justify my deviations from my former style by claiming that I simply had reached a level of higher artistic maturation, prompting me to seek new forms for the enhancement of a more idiosyncratic creative expression. But to my dismay I found that these forms were anything but new. Even the most timorous step towards abstraction, with me only yielded painfully derivative similarities with all too eminent and already too frequently copied paragons, all the way from Brancusi to Epstein. This, in turn, went against my innermost conviction that an artist, in his creative production, must draw solely on his own resources, without any backwards or sidelong glances at the works of others. Once again I heard the dead painter say, "To me, you merely look like someone, who wants to reinvent the wheel."

A milestone in my recollections of this period is the day on which my hair began to fall out. As usual, I awoke at first dawn—I sleep with my window wide open and I still do so at present, down here on the plains. In those days, closer to the heavens by the height of the cliff, I used to spend the nights in the patio of my house and, thus, entirely outdoors. When I opened my eyes, my first sight was that of the fainting stars and of the opalescent hues of the skies. I had dreamt and my awakening, like some blotting paper, absorbed and then extinguished the colorful and lifelike reality of my dream images. They paled into phantoms and vanished, and soon only an echo remained of something vague and tormenting: the irremediability of a futile world. The day was hazy. I went to the precipice and looked in vain for my island. When I returned to the house, Lisa already was up. That was unusual. Ordinarily she slept until all hours, curled up like some animal in the darkest corner of the house. I went to the barrel to draw some water for washing up, but found the barrel empty. Since it was still so early in the day that the mugginess, already heralded by the hazy skies, had not taken hold as yet, I decided to cart the barrel down to the source and fill it. Lisa clung to me, "Don't leave me alone up here!" I didn't mind her coming with me. I always took her with me, whenever I went down to the village.

At the source I met up with the butcher. I was so startled that I asked almost belligerently, "How come you're not in your shop?" "It's Sunday," he replied, smiling with amusement. "I brought a little gift for the signorina." He bent and picked up from among the grass growing around the source a small black-and-white kid goat, not more than a few weeks old, whose legs had been tied up. Lisa took it in her arms. "For a while, you'll still have to feed it on the bottle," the butcher told her, "but later it'll follow you like a pet dog." This cut the ground from under the animosity, which suddenly had swelled up in me against him. I omitted to ask him whether perchance he was looking for any more of those weapons left behind by the Germans. While Lisa delightedly caressed the kid, the butcher fixed me with his gray eyes, as if expecting precisely such a question. Lisa thanked him with a kiss on the cheek. We went on talking about some trifling matters. He turned down our invitation to stay with us for breakfast, as I likewise declined his offer to help us with the carting of the full barrel. We parted with a show of exaggerated cordiality and—so I felt—in a state of tension pregnant with what remained unspoken. "How sweet of him!" Lisa exclaimed time and again. "Whatever could have prompted him to present me with this little pet?" I only could have conjectured an answer and, moreover, I was too heavily engrossed in my thoughts and in my labor of pushing the heavy barrel up the steep slope. Then, when we had arrived at the house and I had passed a wet sponge over my sweaty face, I wiped off my eyebrows. I only realized it after combing my hair and looking in the mirror to understand why the comb had come away so full of hair.

The weeks that followed were not happy ones. Soon I was completely bald. Among the theories I conceived to try to explain this sudden and total alopecia, there was also the one based on the assumption that the butcher could have poisoned the well. But Lisa, who drank the same water and washed herself in it as much as I, showed no ill effects whatever, however closely I watched for such in her. She was of great help to me during that difficult period in that she paid but scant heed to my misfortune. All her attention was concentrated on the kid goat which, indeed, soon followed her around like a lap dog. What fascinated her most in the little pet was its gracefulness in climbing and vaulting over the most scary looking rocks. It would be hopping along merrily along the edge of the cliff, as if the sheer abyss were not yawning a mere finger's breadth away from its dainty, honey-colored hoofs, and it even would bend far over the precipice in order to snatch a mouthful of herbs from some rock fissure. Lisa watched this spectacle with bated breath, as if it were pure magic. This was highly revealing to me and also diverted my mind from my own absurd condition. Whenever she noticed the painful concern this occasioned in me, she would comfort me in her own blunt way: "Now your skull looks like a single gigantic, naked glans," she remarked, "and you no longer have to check whether your real one is free of pimples or eczema. From now on, you'll only have to look in the mirror to make sure."

I bided my time before taking revenge. It was triggered finally by a newspaper excerpt sent to me by an art dealer. He was one of my biggest customers and had arranged a retrospective showing of my works covering the last ten years and including also my latest creations. The newspaper excerpt contained a critical review of the exhibition, and it was scathing. Among other things, it contained the following assessment, "This guileless carver of saintly figures, who hitherto had been adept in combining the traditions of the folkloric art from rural Oberammergau with the sugary soulfulness of a Sulamith Wülfing, now suddenly strives—a latecomer by almost a century—to copy the likes of Ernst Barlach . . ." And so on in the same vein. It seemed to me as if I were hearing the voice of the dead painter. Whoever had murdered her, no one could have had better grounds for it than I.

Sometimes I wondered what would have been her reaction if she had seen me in all my hairlessness; quite probably she would have exclaimed, "Oh my, will you look at that! The latest fashion in penitent's attire?" I could not rid myself of the thought of her. Whatever I did, said or thought, I always imagined how she would comment on it. I became so obsessed with her, that I started to make inquires on my own, in the attempt to find out how she had been killed, but I didn't get very far with these efforts, since I simply lacked the resources to learn about it more than mere hearsay and rumors. Had I shown myself overly eager in my inquiries concerning the event, I myself might have come under suspicion in the village, for the *carabinieri* were still continuing their investigation of the murder. Therefore I limited myself to banal exchanges with the *postino*, who carried the mail, the laundress who did my washing, the owner of the grocery store, which also held the espresso bar, and with the pensioners who, day after day, were sitting in front of it, and I only showed some curiosity myself when the subject was raised by others; after all, it was quite a sensation for the locals, happening—as it did—way before the tourist season. But Southern Italians automatically become tight-lipped where acts of violence, occurring in their midst, are concerned. Nevertheless, I learned a few things I had not known earlier. Needless to say, there circulated also some baseless stories, such as that the painter really had been a German spy, even though this already was contradicted by the simultaneous assertion that her companion, shot together with her, had been an Englishman, specifically a professor at Oxford. It seemed a little hard to believe that the combined intelligence services of Great Britain and West Germany would be using disguised archaeologists to ferret out Italian state secrets, as in Kipling's Nepal of old. Of greater interest to me was the darkly rumored allegation that the butcher had been seen together with the black witch, mostly at night and in his remote olive grove. Even though this fact, in accordance with the unbreakable custom of *omertà*—the collective silence observed whenever some violation of the laws is committed among neighbors—had been carefully concealed from the *carabinieri*, it remained the subject of persistent mutterings among the local inhabitants. It was also said that my friend was still under suspicion, even though it seemed that he had been able to establish such an unshakable alibi for the presumed time of the murder that the investigators had been left no other choice than to look elsewhere for other clues. What these might be, no one knew.

What I really would have liked to know was what possibly could have been the motive for this double murder. It had not been robbery, for none of the belongings of either of the victims had been disturbed. Nor was there the usual incentive for the action of a lunatic, a sexual pervert or a decency fanatic for, surprisingly enough, the scholar and the painter had lived together in total celibacy; while she slept in the trailer, he used to spend the nights outdoors in his sleeping bag. This was one fact one knew for certain—in Italy, every last thing is known about the way of life of foreigners. In any case, this was also how they had been found, each separately shot, she in her folding bed in the camper and he in his sleeping bag under the skies, each with a single clean hole in the forehead. The weapon had been a German army pistol. The chasteness of the murdered painter having thus been established, jealously, too, largely could be eliminated as a motive, a fact that caused me some considerable relief. At the thought of the danger I might have been in, if my sexual relations with the painter had not been of so ephemeral a nature, a cold shiver sometimes still ran down my back.

I saw the butcher as regularly as in the past. He slaughtered on

Mondays. On those days, the ante-room of his narrow shop was draped with mutton halves, hung from sharp hooks in the ceiling and each opened up in the shape of a butterfly, as if for a Rorschach test. The crude rubicondities of those meats, bled dry and ingrained throughout with the yellowish streaks of suet, would have lent themselves as the perfect subject for the still life of some German expressionist painter, such as Lovis Corinth, as well as of some medieval illustrators of infernal scenes. Lambs, with their forelegs crossed as if in prayer, their skulls still covered by finely curled fleece and with their floppy ears covering their eyes, as if shameful of their freshly skinned nakedness, were decked out across the white-tiled counter. "Lucky they! They've got it all behind them! No more loss of hair for them, no more dangerous outings, climbing around in solitary olive groves." I was spouting nonsense and I realized it, but I also knew that the butcher understood all the better to what I alluded. Calmly he asked: "What shall I cut for you?" Nimbly, he began to sharpen his knife on the whetstone. I hesitated: "Maybe two bistecchine for the signorina. As for myself more and more inclined towards vegetarianism, like our murdered friend." That to this opening gambit he did not reply with a single phrase of commiseration for the bitter end of the painter, to me seemed proof of a clear conscience. I watched as he cut the meat. He had placed a large, rosy-red chunk on the hack block in front of him, into which the blade sank without encountering any resistance. He then sliced off a thin slab that peeled down like the petal of a flower, followed by a second one, which gently folded over the first. All this was done swiftly and with grace, almost with a certain tenderness. "*Ecco fatto!*" declared the butcher, placing the two slices between wax-paper, which he then wrapped up in brown paper. In this, too, his hands showed great skill. Such hands would know exactly how to handle a pistol with the requisite precision. Following a sudden impulse I said: "I thought it over; if you have some fresh heart left, I'll take that, too." He brought out a calf's heart from the refrigerator. Its weight lay heavy in his hand. "Shall I carve it up?" he asked. "No, I'd rather do that myself." I watched the figures dancing on the dial of the scales and put the corresponding amount on the counter. "*La signorina sta bene,*" he said more as a statement than a question. "*Sta bene,*" I confirmed. "She's fine and came down with me, but has gone to get some milk for the kid. She's crazy for the little thing." He smiled with satisfaction, showing his white teeth. We nodded to each other. *"Ciao, Sergio! Grazie!" "Grazie a lei, signore!"*

Then, as I was squeezing past the huge carcass of a young steer on my way out, a strange thought occurred to me: it seemed to me as if I were wading waist-high in nothing but flesh. My breath was saturated with it. The weight of all that flesh pressed down on me like a female body in lustful coupling. The haunches of the carcass, hung upside down, gaped monstrously. The grayish-yellow and ruphous cross-hatchings of the rib cage, in which could be seen the porphyry of the kidneys hanging down in pendulous heaviness, grinned at me cavernously. The shallow concavity appeared as if aggressively, even scornfully empty. I thought, "This is the rib cage of what a short while ago has been a live being, a being which, merely a few hours ago, still breathed in the fragrance of the meadows and the blueness of the skies in all their wide spaciousness, breathed it all in and out in steamy-warm snorts, taking in the whole big world in a single deep breath. A young steer in the fullness of its powers: an almost mythical being. But now, there, where the whole world had been encompassed by each intake of breath, there is nothing but emptiness—and that is the absolute, the final truth. There is no other truth than that emptiness. As I was thinking this, I was suddenly overcome with the simultaneous certitude that it had been no other than the butcher who had shot the painter and why this had to have happened. Such sudden revelations are not that rare but, in general, one hardly pays any attention to them.

The girl Lisa waited for me in front of the espresso bar of the grocer's shop. Together, we climbed up to my house on the cliff. On the way—we were barely at mid-height—she took my hand, as if wanting to be led like a tired child. "Barlach is a great artist, isn't he?" she said, half in question. "I have no clear recollection of his works, but they seemed to be endowed with a kind of monumental quality, something of the early medieval, don't you think? Something Romanesque. There's some article, I think by Worringer, on the subject of monumentality, if I'm not mistaken." Quite obviously she had found the newspaper excerpt with the review of my work. I had not given it to her to read, not perhaps because of wounded vanity, but rather because I was hardly interested in her opinions. I had had more than enough of such art-theoretical gibberish in my exchanges with the dead painter (and continued to have these in the form of monologues). Lisa's attempts at comforting me were an irritation. Not only because of their naïve clumsiness, but even more so because they clearly indicated that this girl was in love with me. And thereby she lost for me her elf-like airiness. She became earthbound. Carnal. She made me think of my mother. The only thing I had admired in my mother had been her inability to love—she had never shown such a feeling, either to me or to any of her innumerable beaus. In the coldness of her heart she had had something majestic. This was the legacy she had left me. Without it, I would have been nothing at all. What really had vexed me in that critical review was the imputation of "sugary soulfulness à la Sulamith Wülfing." That was a gross misinterpretation. If my Blessed Virgins were so popular, it was precisely because of their chaste severity. And, if lately, I had sought even more simplified forms, it was so as to exalt further that character of loftiness, of sublimity beyond the earthly. Because I was so deeply in thought and remained silent, the girl Lisa also fell silent, but continued to hold my hand. I left it in hers almost out of aversion.

The little goat kid was so used to the house that, each time we went down to the village, it would follow us only as far as the edge of the *macchia*, the growth of brushwood and crippled trees which ended just above the source. The rocky ground above was its very own domain, in which it could romp and frolic at will. The little animal had very sharp instincts and would sense our return already from far away. Usually, it would come bleating to our welcome even before we had reached the source. Lisa always had a handful of particularly redolent herbs as a greeting. But on that day, the little goat failed to meet us. In vain did Lisa call for it. She had named Griseldis, a rather extravagant name, which to me seemed less poetic than rather typical of petit bourgeois sentimentality. (Perhaps the dead painter hadn't given me my full due, after all . . .) In any case, no trace could be found of Griseldis.

Lisa looked for the kid goat for a full two days and, in so doing, even forgot about her own acrophobia. So as to check whether her darling might not be standing on some projection above the vertiginous abyss, from where—despite all its agility—it could not regain the safety of the rock plateau, Lisa ventured all the way to the edge of the drop and even bent over it in such daredevil abandon that I feared she might at any moment lose her balance and tumble all the way down to her death.

I need admit that I, too, missed the pet goat. Its droll hopping around on its clumsily graceful stick legs had brought to our setting—a rather barren one, save for the abundance of surrounding blooms—a kind of Böcklinesque vitality. It exemplified for us to what an extent the landscape in which we lived was impregnated with the bucolic myths of the past. The yellow eyes of Griseldis were those of satyrs and presumably also those of the great Pan himself. Its attachment to Lisa was touching. Lisa usually went about barefoot, but her whereabouts at all times were heralded by the sounds of the little hoofs tripping over the stones, for Griseldis followed at her heels by no more than the width of a hand. I found the half-eaten and rotting carcass of the poor thing after almost a week had passed, at the edge of the macchia, not far from the source. It probably had been torn to bits by a band of roving dogs; it was almost too large for a fox who, moreover, would have dragged it into its earth. Of course, crows had gotten to it, too, so that the delicate black-and-white fleece hung down in rags; underneath, maggots pullulated. But the head with the golden eyes, now dulled and half closed and from which ants trickled down like red tears, was still intact. Lisa kissed the black lips, cleft under the nostrils.

What struck me as extraordinary was that Lisa's sudden lack of vertigo endured. Now she would pass the precipice without paying it any heed, at times walking all the way to the edge and looking out at sea. Quite obviously, this also meant for her (as well as for me) the simultaneous loss of this special erotic stimulation. Our copulations became slack through habit. I was about to intimate to her that the time had come for her return home. Autumn made itself felt, and however mild the winter might be down here in the South, it hardly could be expected to be spent in an unheatable stone house by a comfortably brought-up girl from Münster in Westphalia. Lisa, however, made no preparation for such a return. This surprised me all the more as I treated her in anything but a loving manner. I was constantly irritated. I found myself repugnant in my overall bareness. Her repeated comment that my polished skull looked like an enormous penis in erection, now triggered in me outbursts of fury. Although I told myself that I had to get accustomed to my appearance, I had banished all mirrors from the house. I believe that Lisa nevertheless kept a small one hidden in her suitcase, the one she had retrieved at the last moment from the tour bus. It contained all her belongings. Up to now, this modest piece of luggage had appeared to me as epitomizing her uprootedness; a readily movable container for the shabby trash that perhaps a circus artiste might carry along in her roamings: a silver wig and a tinseled corset, the padded slippers and the Japanese parasol of a tightrope acrobat, who weightlessly glides each evening among shimmering, varicolored lights, here today and God knows where tomorrow. All this my poetic fantasy had attributed to the little suitcase, whenever I saw it sitting in some corner of our sleeping quarters, half open and sloppily filled with summery clothes and cheap travel souvenirs. But now this inconspicuous carry-all suddenly seemed to grow roots and sink these stubbornly deeper into my abode. And what I saw proliferating from those roots were the clinging lianas of love.

This love, in view of my condition, Lisa adorned additionally with the nimbus of Samaritan compassion. She belonged good and well to that species of women who, in medieval times, were wont to lick the wounds of the plague-ridden. It made my stomach turn over whenever I recalled how she had kissed the cleft lips of Griseldis's rotting corpse. Add to all this that nothing I carved really worked out to my satisfaction. This, too, I held against Lisa. Her presence bothered me like one of those persistently returning flies, which one cannot shoo away. She had become a mute widow in her grief over an animal which, in any case and had it lived, soon would have lost the gracefulness of its youth, growing into an angular sway-backed she-goat with pendulous udders and crooked horns. Lisa, too, seemed to have lost all her charm. Instead of her former vivacious drollery, she now affected a kind of meek humility, with which she burdened me as if it were of my own making. While heretofore she had left me alone to my work, she now was coming at every dang hour of the day into the studio, where she would then squat down silently in a corner and watch me work. But my furiously concentrated carving could not hold her attention for long; soon her glance would slide away from me and into a dull nowhere in front of her feet, her hands in her lap, demonstrating for me what hitherto had been the main subject of my artistic endeavor: a *mater dolorosa* grieving for a goat. Once, she raised her head to ask: "Tell me, what was she like, that painter, who owned the house before you?" She knew, of course, that the painter had been murdered, although I had avoided speaking of it in anything more than a passing reference.

Even so, it was startling that she spoke of this, as if she had been able to read my thoughts. True, I was already beyond the phase in which I had gone on all the time discussing my artistic tenets with the dead woman in self-torturing monologues. Now my argumentations with myself plumbed deeper: I debated the obsessive thought that the real cause of my crisis might reside in my very existence in this particular location, above the cliff and in a landscape which was so contradictory to my German origins. This was pagan soil. The old myths still lived here in terrifying immediacy. Here even Christendom had become invested with pagan colors and a pagan richness of forms. I came from a protestant country. That nevertheless I had selected the Madonna as the great subject of my creative strivings originated in the mythic traditions of Germandom itself, which even a Luther had been unable to uproot entirely. This was a mysticism thoroughly different from the heritage of the pagan pantheon, which here survived in the swarms of innumerable Catholic saints. The German Mother of God was not that goddess of fertility who, albeit converted to Christianity, tore to pieces her son Zagreus, so as to spread his flesh as fertilizer into the furrow of ploughed fields. Even in the spiritualized representation of a Raphael, this was altogether another Madonna than the one Mathias Grünewald depicted for the altar in Colmar. But one requires sharp eyes to recognize this, I told myself, particularly when appearances lead one to believe the opposite. I pictured myself defending these theses against the murdered painter—confusedly, without any doubt, and flustered by her repeated taunts of "Oh my!" and "Oh, come on now!" But that wasn't the core of my problem. What mattered was that I had begun to doubt myself. I had begun doubting in me what the dead painter once had called the "artistic hardness factor." "To cut glass, you need a diamond, *capisci*?" she had said. I understood her now all too well. I thought of the knife of the butcher and how unswervingly it sank into the pieces of meat. And I wondered whether I, too, would be capable of shooting a pistol bullet into the head of a sleeper.

The weather turned nasty. It seemed to me as if months had passed since last I had been able to see my island. Lisa shivered in her shabby summery frocks. I made as if I did not notice it and showed no inclination of buying her anything warmer. She had appropriated an old wool cardigan of mine, full of holes, in which she wrapped herself like some scullery maid. Her submissiveness only served to further envenom my animosity towards her. I decided to put her to the test. Much earlier, when such images still served to arouse Lisa's erotic instincts, I had told her of the first emperor of Haiti, Henri Christophe who, fearing that Napoleon may reclaim his rebellious island and send a punitive expedition to subdue his people once more, had a Swiss architect build for him a fortress, spiked with cannons as the back of a hedgehog and located on the highest peak of a mountain shaped like a sugar cone, whence he had a fine view of the entire coastline. But he waited in vain for the arrival of his Corsican antagonist, who had more pressing matters to worry about. Meanwhile Henri Christophe kept a strong garrison for his protection and had them exercise diligently on the flat roof of the castle. When he realized finally that all this expenditure was superfluous, since Napoleon already was exiled to Saint Helena, he ordered his troops to march over the edge of the citadel, where the walls fell flush with the vertical drop of the mountain slope. His soldiers obeyed without hesitation; squadron after squadron, men after men, fell to their death, until not a single man was left. "Love requires absolute obedience," I told Lisa. "Would you be ready to walk over the edge for me?" She calmly replied, "Perhaps, if it had to be." I then said, "That doesn't count. Not because it has to be, but merely because I ask you to?" Wrapped in the wool cardigan, she cowered in a corner. "Probably, if you were to ask me to do so," she said. "I'm no longer afraid." "Not at all?" "Not at all." "So prove it!"

She rose and went outside. I followed. She went towards the edge of the cliff. "Not like that," I called after her. "That's too easy. You have to close your eyes and walk backwards. Trusting in me that I'll call you back before it's too late. But also in the full knowledge that this will be done only at the last, the very last moment." She turned around to face me, closed her eyes and, step by step, walked backwards like a sleepwalker, ever closer to the sheer drop. Not even I could stand this for very long and so I called out "Stop!" when a few steps still separated her from the edge. She came to a halt, looked back over her shoulder to measure the distance left and shrugged contemptuously. Then, with the same somnambulistic gait, she walked towards me, her eyes fixed unswervingly in mine. When she stood in front of me, she spat squarely in my face. She disappeared the next day, together with her little suitcase. The wool cardigan she left behind.

In that year, winter set in with stormy days of rain. Because it was a nuisance to climb down to the village in such weather, I got into the habit of buying my supplies for several weeks at a time. I bought my meat in huge pieces, which I had to hang, since I did not have a refrigerator. Because I feared that, if hung in the kitchen, it would attract all kinds of varmint, I hung it in the studio, where it surrounded me while I worked. Also, air circulated better in the spaciousness of the studio. Meat keeps fresh in air longer than one might assume and, in fact, gets more tender, as well as tastier in the process. Its increasingly strong smell filled my whole house. I became slowly aware that I was developing a neurotic obsession. It would have been much simpler for me to live as a vegetarian, alike the murdered painter, or at least on a half-vegetarian diet, eating the many Italian pastas and various canned foods. But I insisted on meat. What I really enjoyed was to cut it. It was at that time that I procured for myself, with the help of the butcher, a complete set of professionally sharp knives. From the stump of an olive tree, I fashioned a regular butcher's block, on which I practiced cutting meat with relish and with growing skill. Of all meats, heart keeps the longest and also lends itself best to carving.

I made so little progress with my work that soon I abandoned it altogether. Whatever I attempted turned out as conscious or unconscious imitation, as nothing but derivative botchwork. I may say of myself without presumption that I am a highly expert craftsman. I know all the tricks of the trade—by which I mean all those sleights-of-hand and deceptive devices of the profession, by which an artist is able to raise his creation to the level of a "work of art," that is those minor, last-minute finishing touches, which can endow a workpiece of already fortuitously high quality with the ultimate luster of a fated stroke of genius. The artistic vision is not something that is given *a priori*. It is something which is innate in the given work material and emanates from it. It is embodied in that subtle manipulation itself with which you, the artist, are able to ease it forth from the material. The slightest slip of the hand may chase it away forever. Be conscious at all times of the danger that the smallest error in execution can unmask the fraud you are about to commit. Then you may be fortunate enough to bring out in your work that ideal form which, universally, is innate in every concrete object in this world. But if that good fortune is not granted to you, form disintegrates in your very hands; that which is to be formed reverts to the amorphous. And if you use fraudulent tricks in trying to arrest this disintegration, this falling apart, the imperfectly formed turns into a travesty, a mockery of the ideal form.

This is precisely what happened to me now in all my attempts. My fakery became obvious as soon as I set my carving knife to the wood. And yet I knew that such faking was essential and that without it, no work of art can come into being. What matters is the quality of the fakery, I told myself. I had spoken often with the dead painter of that marvelous parable in Kleist's *Puppet Master*: The way around the world that need be traveled in order to attain, by way of the unquestioning certitude of the naïve artist, the sovereignty of true masterdom, a way that need lead through the self-perception of consciousness. The more clear-sighted you are in committing your fraud, the more legitimate it will turn out to be. The one who knows the ways of the world will take possession of the material, so as to transubstantiate its essence into form. The faker is elevated to the rank of the high priest. But for that I lacked the required consecration. Heretofore I had merely faked my art and, in fake humility, I had invoked tradition as my legitimization. This no longer would do. All that the past had bequeathed was to be avoided—unless it were quoted in irony. The "ideal form" that can be brought forth from the material in most cases already exists; it has been extracted already long ago from the material. Art no longer has a valid subject—except itself. And I told myself that I had to apply this insight to my own work; that now that I had become conscious of my true calling as artist, I was duty-bound to consider my own self as the essential workpiece; that it was the form, innate in that very same self, that would determine my rank as an artist and that, therefore, if I wanted to endow my fakery with that magic, I had to bring it forth from that self, which alone could raise it to the mystery of the true artistic masterpiece.

The creative crisis of an artist is too fatuous a subject to be brought to the attention of the world at large. Fortunately, I was in no position to do so, even had I wanted to. There were times when I laughed in fury at myself, while staring into the weaving and roiling grayness outside, into this stormy turmoil, cross-hatched by rainy streaks and made up of clumps of dark clouds filling the skies above the cliff and over a sea, discolored and diseased, braking out in leprous whitecaps. I scoffed at my own loneliness, at the impotent frailty of my wrestling with the angel of art—I, the carver before God, the carver of holiness, who knew no other God than the one hidden in a piece of wood, that God who now demanded that I give Him form with my hands, those hands which He had failed to bless, with a spirit that was unclean and had been granted neither innocence nor divine inspiration. What ate at me was the mordant derision of the murdered painter. I still could hear her mocking interjections of "Oh my!" and "Oh, come on now!" whenever I spoke of the present sad state of art, in which recognition only is granted to self-aggrandizers of their own individuality, the solipsistic mayflies of ephemeral fads, who merely create singularities, but nothing lasting and of permanent value. Even the greatest craftsmanship no longer suffices—so I had asserted—to provide a work with the quality of uniqueness, a creation out of nothingness, a feat reserved merely to a handful of magicians: Duchamp sees in a bottle rack "the fortuitously innate ideal form of the workpiece" and declares it to be art, disdaining even the minutest alteration, which would allow some bicycle clips or some radiator tubes to yield up their aesthetic content . . .

In fact, I no longer knew whether I actually had said all this to the painter, while she was still alive, or whether I simply went on ranting now merely for the benefit of her insubstantial shade. The grayness into which I stared, was thinly populated: neither with the butcher, nor with the girl Lisa had I ever had a conversation worth recapitulating or one to be continued in spirit; for this I was entirely dependent on the dead painter and her opinions, as well as her derision now began to become my own. I could not claim that my crisis in reality was a religious one—not even the secularized parody of such a one, the carnival costuming of a crisis of faith—without the painter (but now, in truth, it was I myself) seeing through such lofty subterfuge and nailing me down on it in the full realization of my inadequacy and of my impotence. She dismissed me with the same contempt with which, after my initial failure during our "fall into sin," she had lifted my flaccid penis between two fingers, only to let it drop back in mocking derision. What good could it do me to speak of my strivings to depict the Mother of God in a truly new manner, a synthesis of Raphael and Grünewald, as an offspring of Demeter and Kali, bearer of God and of Man, whose fruit was nothing but a naked worm, helplessly exposed to ultimate rotting and serving in this world for nothing more than as the fertilizer for all growth. The sheer presence in my mind of the dead painter unmasked all this as the pretentious gibberish it was; and my attempts to create with the carving knife a symbolic image of an Arch-Mother—something on the order of a female body, such as is seen, for instance, in Cycladic or African sculptures: the torso, rising from the monstrous fleshy mass of the hips, like an axe blade stuck into a heart—these attempts floundered on my realization that I lacked the power to go a step further than those grand models, be it merely in empathic resonance. I lacked the magic. I lacked what the dead painter had called "the specific hardness." Had I been capable of letting the girl Lisa walk over the edge of the cliff, I might have had no need to doubt either my calling or my validity as an artist.

And yet I knew that I had no fear of any abysses, of any depths. I did not lack in hardness against myself. I had heard of an artist in America who had exemplified the desperate straights of the modern artist in an act of terrifying immediacy. He surrounded himself with high-voltage wires in such a way that their discharge would be triggered by the slightest of his movements, causing his death by electric shock. It was the most daring of all works of art, one pushing to the limits of sheer horror an art left with no other subject than itself. I started to toy with the idea that I might use the butcher in an experiment of similar daring. I held the butcher in my power. By giving him something to understand, how easy it would be for me to break his supposedly airtight and irrefutable alibi, I might induce him to do away with me as a potentially lethal witness. Nor did he have to obtain another pistol for this purpose; his knives would serve him just as well. Or even my own. The thought of it aroused me. The overwhelming reek of meat, in which I dwelled, somehow intoxicated me. It seemed to me almost as if I were breathing my own blood. I climbed down to the village and straightaway went to see the butcher. "I have something important to discuss with you," I told him. "It can't be done here. Come to see me after you've closed shop and don't tell anyone where you're going. Be sure to come. It's of paramount importance to you." Then I went to the grocery store, bought a bottle of *grappa*, drank my coffee and exchanged some banalities with the pensioners, who now had withdrawn to the warmth of the interior, mostly talk about the bad weather which culminated in the remark that, well, yes, what could you expect; it was winter once more after all. After which I climbed back up to my house.

Even before visiting the butcher, I had sharpened and polished all my knives and had spread them out on the chopping block. Large pieces of meat hung from the low timbered ceiling, for I had secured the same needle-sharp, S-shaped hooks used in slaughterhouses, so that the room indeed resembled a butcher's shop. I pushed the table into the center of the room, placed the bottle and two glasses on in, and waited. Darkness came early and abruptly at that time of the year; it would be night by the time the butcher closed shop. I lit my carbide lamp. Its harsh white light made the ruddy shades of the meat look poisonous. The colors of Grünewald. The girl Lisa had spoken of primary-symptom-colored raspberries. Rosy pinks on a cyclamen-color background. The rose and the lily, the flowers of the Madonna. I started to drink. I drank glass after glass, but at first took care to leave the bottle half full. I drink seldom and the hard liquor soon went to my head. It got later and later and the butcher didn't come. I passed the halfway mark on the bottle. I thought of the painter, who in this very place had rutted with the butcher. A coupling of titans, so different from my own piteous attempt at assertion after my initial failure. I thought of the girl Lisa and of the kiss she implanted on the black lips of the rotting kid goat. The butcher still failed to appear and my irritation grew. I felt rage rising in me. The thought occurred to me that I was not to be cheated. My thirst to the outermost boundaries and beyond was not to be brought to naught in so shabby a manner. I had to do without the butcher. My impatience with this whole situation became such, that I felt my penis hardening in erection. I opened my trousers and took it out. There it was, proudly rigid and full, overhung and crowned by the mat lustrous silkiness of the glans: my true I, scepter of my self-esteem, my guidepost. In it, my very being was striving forth to its utmost; in it was to be found the seat of my ideal essence. It is on this workpiece that I would achieve the apotheosis of all my carvings, my sculptures of holiness. I went to the chopping block, calmly placed my penis on top of it, and cut if off with a single stroke of my sharpest knife.

The *carabinieri* were the ones who saved me from bleeding to death. They had come to interrogate me once more. It had somehow become known that the butcher had called on me in the morning after the murder. I swore that, instead, it had been the day before and that I had thrown into the sea the pistol, whose alleged possession had brought the butcher under suspicion. I was able to substantiate this with a notation in my calendar. But before all that, I had been brought to the hospital. After my release, I left the house on the cliff. Now I live in the lowlands, in the marshes around Worpswede, where once Rilke and Paula Modersohn-Becker had lived. I have given up carving. I always had a bit of money of my own and, in addition, my sculptures of the Madonna, especially my late ones, have become so famous, that I get very high prices for the few remaining pieces I had kept. I live the life of a recluse. The bareness of my skull I cover under a hat. This bareness unduly attracts women. Generally, I am considered a maverick and a loner. Children and young people find me weird. My dogs are feared by all.

Translated from the German by H.F. Brock de Rothermann.

LETTERS

Irate in Philly

I recently bought both of the late Robert Bingham's books, a copy of *Open City* Number Ten, and the entire output of Donald Antrim and Sam Lipsyte. If the purpose of your *Open City* is to turn people on to brilliant American writers: Congratulations, goal met. I thank you for turning me on to those truly good writers.

If, on the other hand, you are meant to be a "positive creative nuisance"—an edgy, truly inclusive compendium of American voices you have failed. In my estimate and many others, the most potent and accomplished poets of our time are hip-hop performers like Common, Pharoah [sic] Monche, Talib Kweli, and Black Thought, alongside spoken-word folks like the astonishing Ursula Rucker. When rich, privileged kids who went to Brown (who cares?) are elevated and lauded at the expense of other equally or more gifted wordsmiths who have worked against far greater odds to achieve their goals, something is clearly fucked up. Open City my ass. "Open" means you are rich and white and did good drugs in the past twenty years. "City" means you live in Manhattan and you bought your loft with your Trustafundian money. I see, it's a code . . .

The vestigial mental apartheid code that created the first colored drinking fountain is alive and well in your stylish offices and in your tacit attitude toward language and who judges its value (namely you and your rich poser friends in a giant circle jerk of self-congratulation). Someday, when I can pick up *Open City* and find the poetry of Big Rich Medina next to Thomas Beller's latest story, you will have actually achieved the real victory, not the arrogant myopia and Pyrrhic victory you currently enjoy.

Publish this fucker.

Aaron Luis Levinson
Philadelphia, America